The Locust Fields

To TRISH
ALL THE BOT
AnD I HotF You
STill mJoy'z
Paul Davies
30/5/19

Book 3

Death's Rising

With thanks to Lesley

Prologue

"THIS IS STUPID!" Peabody yelled, "THE WHOLE IDEA IS MAD!" The other two men in the large hut said nothing. Erwin sat on a small three legged stool at the far end of the hut, just inside the shadows, masking the slight smile that broke his lips. He was Prince Tagan's advisor, and had joined the army of Greater Longmans to find out useful information about the Destroyer's creatures, but this had so far been fruitless, he had now decided to return to Kleve with Peabody's soldiers.

Major Gladstone was Peabody's second in command a Mounted Marine who despite being of equal rank to Peabody, and having more soldiers, had submitted willingly to Peabody's authority. He slowly walked over and picked up the letter which Peabody had thrown onto the floor, flattening it out he began to read it to himself. Peabody said nothing, he walked to the open door and looked outside.

Before him was the full activity of an army in the last moments of preparation to move. The first rays of sunlight now just broke through an overcast sky illuminating figures hurrying along with their tasks, a few raised voices shouted orders, but there was no cursing or swearing associated with any normal army preparing to march, Peabody's army was different in so many ways.

"Congratulations Sir, you've been promoted to Colonel, the Field Marshal cannot be that upset with the report that we sent him?" Gladstone said. The report was the reason they were there, to find information to help the Allied Army defeat the creatures outside Kleve, they had found nothing useful, but when looking for witnesses to the earlier battle which had taken place in the area, came across a village full of just women, in an effort to help the women protect themselves from bandits attacking them, Peabody and his men had begun to train the women how to fight, they had proved themselves very good as soldiers. Now the villagers had requested they go along with the army and join them in the fight, Peabody had agreed, but was now having second thoughts!

"Don't you see?" Peabody said, his arms open wide in explanation, "when we get to Kleve we will be the laughing stock of the army, most of our 'soldiers' are women!"

"May I ask?" Erwin said from the shadows, "When we wrote the report three quarters of our army were women, and they still are, what has changed?"

"I don't know, it just seems wrong now, it's all too real."

"Well, real or not, we are where we are, so I would suggest we just get on with it." Erwin said as he stood and walked to the entrance to join Peabody looking out at the activity, "it seems a good time to start," then nodding to both Peabody and Gladstone he walked over to the head of the waiting line of horses, soldiers and carts.

"Well, Sir, I suggest we join them," Gladstone said, "and we really need to do something about your rank Colonel, you're still showing as a Major." Together the two officers followed Erwin to the head of the line.

The last of the preparations were just being completed as they came to a huddle of officers and none commissioned officers discussing any last problems. Satisfied with everything, they moved off to their posts, Peabody went to mount his horse, taking his reins from Willow who was already mounted.

"Is everything alright?" Willow asked when he was settled.

"Yes, but I think we are a bit late to get to Kleve, the Destroyer's creatures have already left." Peabody said with a smile towards her.

"Well that's a good thing isn't it? If the creatures have gone surely the war is over?"

"No I don't think it is. The letter from the Field Marshal did not say they had defeated the creatures just that they had left!"

A bugle call cut though the silence of the early morning signalling the start of the long march to Kleve, they were an unusual army following in the wake of the Greater Longmans' Army who had left the day before, both heading towards an uncertain future.

Chapter 1

The view from the small balcony onto the inner palace gardens was beautiful. The well cut lawns and flower beds of all colours made a lovely foreground to the striking blood red sunset which enveloped the palace and surrounding city. Tim drank in the view and the scent from the climbing rose beside him. He was just thinking of how his life had changed, his memory drifting back to his childhood with Aaron when a slight tap on the main apartment door bought him back to reality. Turning to walk inside and answer the door, he watched as it slowly and hesitantly opened.

No servant would be so nervous about entering a room, and anyone he knew would have no fear from him! Quickly he glanced where his bow and a quiver of arrows lay, silently he grabbed the bow and an arrow, taking the strain on the bow string he aimed towards the door. Slowly, very slowly he edged towards a good clear shooting position, the door had not moved.

With a dry mouth and racing heart, Tim tried to control his breathing, taking one slow deliberate step at a time until whatever was behind the partially opened door was revealed.

The door swung open, "EEEEEEKKKK!!" Megan screamed as she came into sight of Tim's bow, "WHAT ARE YOU DOING?"

Quickly lowering his bow, heart now seemingly trying to pound out of his chest, Tim gasped, "Megan, what, what are you doing sneaking around like that, I could have killed you!"

"I hardly think I was sneaking around," Megan replied, now entering the room and sitting herself on one of the three settees in the room, "and what do you have to be afraid of here in the palace? The creatures have all gone."

Tim smiled, putting down his bow he went and sat beside her. How could she know it was in those very palace corridors that the creatures had tried to kill him? He now, began to look at her as if for the first time since she had opened the door. She wore a long silver dress, low cut and off her shoulders, her hair was up slowing off her neck and the diamond necklace, she looked totally different from all the other times he had seen her.

"You look beautiful, where did you get the dress from?"

"Oh these," Megan smiled, "do you like it, the Queen gave it to me as she said I did not seem to have anything to wear for dinner, and yes we are invited to dine with them. But first, I want you to talk to me."

8

"Talk to you, what do you mean?" Tim replied, a confused look covering his face.

"Yes," Megan said, "We have never really talked about what is going on, how it all started. I want to know how you Tim, ended up here, The Champion Lord in a palace hunted by creatures and commanding an army of other creatures."

"Well," said Tim sitting back, "where do I start? I suppose the best place is on a dark night in a field in the village where I come from, Harmer Hill, its right on the western side of Mercia. We had heard rumours of raiders killing and stealing sheep all along the border, so Ananaba our Constable had decided to set a trap for them.

Ananaba was a good friend to Aaron and me, and the youngest Constable in the district, he also knew what he was doing so when he asked for help to lay a trap, most of the village's men folk turned out to help."

"Sorry," Megan interrupted, "Whose Aaron?" Tim stood and slowly began to walk around the room, stopping occasionally to look at Megan to see if she was following.

"Aaron, Aaron was my brother, who you will hear a lot more of as I tell you my story," Tim continued, "It was quite late and dark that night, we had a small herd of sheep in a field surrounded on three sides by woods, in the woods all the villagers had hid with our bows and arrows, just waiting. Then we saw the creatures for the first time, we had never seen anything like them in our lives before, and they were racing straight towards us. We tried to shoot arrows at them as fast as possible but they were moving too fast and there were too many of them, just as they burst into the woods by us the night sky was full of thousands of arrows, all falling and killing the creatures. It was then we realised Ananaba had been injured and I first met Prince Tagan, Lord Cogan, Mortimer, Death and of course Faith. To cut a long story short Aaron and I seemed to be the target of the creatures and in order to save our village we had to leave with Prince Tagan and his army, Faith and Mortimer came with us."

"It was on the way to Kleve we were attacked by the creatures and Me, Faith and Mortimer became separated from the rest. It was very frightening as we were being chased by wolves and the creatures, it was Death that saved us. I don't know too much of the rest of the journey as I had been injured and was hallucinating for a lot of the time. At Kleve we eventually met Aaron and the rest of them, Aaron had been hidden as a Lancer and Prince Tagan asked me if I would act as a decoy for him, they seemed to think Aaron was the key to everything, but they didn't know why. Well I agreed and therefore I became the Queen's messenger."

"I must say it was quite exciting, I was given some new very posh clothes, a good horse and a sword. Captain Trumpeter, who you met, became my tutor in the art of swordsmanship, my body guard and most of all, he became my very good friend."

"I was also tutored by Baroness Heartfelt who taught me how to talk, behave and even walk like a gentleman," he stopped abruptly when he looked across to where Megan was sitting, a smile all over her face.

In response to his questioning look, she said, "And she did a very good job too, I will have to thank her if I ever meet her."

"Yes, well," Tim continued, "after we had a report that one of our armies had been destroyed in the south, Prince Tagan, Mortimer, Avtur, Faith's brother, who had come to help us, and Aaron went in search of The Seeker, who they believed would give them some answers."

"I didn't realise Avtur had come here, but if I remember correctly quite a few Fairies left at the same time." Megan said, almost to herself. Tim listened but said nothing, he had not really known Avtur that well.

He then said, "At the same time a very large army was sent to confront the creatures, I believe they too were destroyed some time later. But what I do know is I continued my training and one day, quite soon, was given my first mission. It was on this mission that I came across the cave which held the Guardian, but I did not know that then, it just seemed like a lot of very large dead insects, with old weapons and armour, I had no idea at the time how that would change my life!"

"We knew Prince Tagan had returned to our lands, to a place they called Mountain Hold, with a very large army and Lord Cogan had joined up with them to fight the creatures on their terms. Then one day I was called to the gardens, which was being used as a landing and departing place for the fairies to meet a new creature which seemed to be on our side, it was Aaron. When they had talked to the Seeker, something had happened and Aaron had transformed into the Golden Griffin, he explained to me how and why, but he looked fantastic, I was impressed."

"That was the last time I saw him, he flew back to the army and I stayed in Kleve doing my duty, which very soon was to ride hard to the army to tell them that Kleve was being surrounded by the creatures. I arrived just at the end of the battle, the battle which we had beaten the creatures, but in which Aaron had been killed!" Tim stopped and took a sip from a glass Megan handed him, giving reassuring hold to his hand at the same time, Tim drank his wine as he controlled his emotions, the death of Aaron still felt raw, and this was the first time he had really talked about it, putting down the glass Tim began passing the room again to continue relaying his story.

"The very next day Prince Tagan realised we could not defeat the creatures without others help and the others were

Griffins, Aaron may have been the last Golden Griffin, but we had to find other Griffins to see if they could help us. So Prince Tagan, Faith, Mortimer, me and Captains Trumpeter and Johnson, with some Trog Light Horse, set out to find Griffins, our first destination was to go to Harmer Hill my home village to see if I could find any answers."

"On the way there we went through a lot of burnt out towns and villages, showing what the creatures were capable of, but in one town we met an officer who told us what happened to all the people from the destroyed villages, as we had seen no trace of survivors. He said they had found some caves where the survivors were herded into and then forced into cocoons, emerging later as fully grown creatures! This inspired us to continue our journey, at ever greater speed."

"We came to Harmer Hill my home village," Tim continued, his face showing the pain of remembering, "I saw and spoke to my father, he was dying. He told me about his life, how he had found and cared for Aaron when he was vulnerable, and therefore lived for a very, very long time, he was a Griffin friend, but when his Griffin was killed, he would die as well. He told me I was not a Griffin friend and that I had my own path and destiny to follow, but he did not know what that was yet. After my father died the village was attacked by creatures and we had to flee. We left the Light Horse behind with Captain Johnson to help the village, but made our own way to find the Griffins."

"On a dark snowy wind swept night in an abandoned village all our lives changed! We had settled down for the night, I think Trumpeter had just taken over the watch, when suddenly the whole place seemed to be filled with very large savage wolves. I saw one lunging at Faith who was still asleep, and Trumpeter jump towards it, sword held high as he was about to strike, then suddenly a brilliant light and a flash, Trumpeter and Faith had vanished into thin air, the wolf dazed, stopped it's attack, but then saw me. Fear and dread began to build inside my stomach as I gathered my belongings and drew my sword. I never knew why I had gathered together my belongings, when it was clear I would have to fight for my life - but I did. I then had an overwhelming feeling inside me as if my body would burst open with it. I was in a silent panic, rooted to the spot I stood on, unable to move, as this large wolf slowly, deliberately advanced towards me, I could feel its breath on my face, but was unable to move. Then it happened - a sudden burst of pain and sickness. The feelings of rushing wind and great movement, like traveling through the air - then nothing! I had closed my eyes, and when I opened them I realised I had moved, I was clueless as to how and where I had travelled, but now I seemed to be in the middle of a desert."

"Death came to me as I tried to find my way out of the desert, I asked him many questions but got very few answers, one of the main questions which had been uppermost in my mind was, Aaron could only be killed by an arrow made from pure gold. No one could make an arrow from pure gold and be able to shoot it from a bow high enough to reach the altitude required. The only answer was that magic must have been used, so the next question was - by who?"

"When I arrived at, what I now know was the Dark Forest I was convinced I was in the place of magic and someone must have some knowledge of how this was done. Then I met Captain Trumpeter again and Titus, one of your Fairies who had gone to help the fight against the Destroyer's creatures. Titus told me that when he had heard the call to return, he and all the other Fairies had obeyed, however, since returning the Fairies all seemed to have met untimely deaths. All the deaths were supposedly accidents, but Titus was sure there was something more sinister to it!"

"That is when I decided to leave the Dark Forest with Captain Trumpeter and Titus, Faith would not join us despite my asking and explaining my fears, but she asked me to bring you along with us."

"Do you have any regrets, bringing me along?" Megan asked.

Tim did not answer, giving a quick smile which never reached his eyes, he said, "I realised we could not walk across the desert, but had a feeling I could ask for help from Griffins. So I did, and as you know two came to help us, they reviled to me about being the Champion Lord, and then I knew which way my path must take. So when we arrived at the army I knew Captain Trumpeter and myself must go back to the cave in which we had found the sleeping insect creature, the Griffins had said they had heard a voice calling on the wind, and needed to respond to the call, I thought that could be Tagan and Mortimer, so intending to leave you with the army Me and Trumpeter would follow our destiny."

"Like me staying with the army was going to happen!" Megan cut in.

"You know we were attacked by the creatures and Captain Trumpeter killed, but you were able to fly to the cave and get help, from what we now know to be the Guardian."

"Well as you know Tagan had been the voice on the wind which the Griffins had heard, and he and Mortimer returned with twenty five Griffins. We had the Guardian Army and joined with the Allied Army we fought the Destroyer's creatures outside Kleve. But far from being beaten the creatures after fighting very hard and inflicting many losses on us, just left, crossing the desert to the Dark Forest which the now surround. I have no idea where we go from here, but I do not for a moment think it's over!"

Chapter 2

Faith hurried up the stairway with all the dignity which she could muster. It was not considered proper to fly in the Dark Wood, the part of the Dark Forest in which the Fairies lived. Faith the Royal Princess was not going to give anyone an excuse to criticize her.

The stairs were narrow and twisted following the inner trunk of the tallest tree of the Dark Forest. It gave an undisturbed panoramic view of the entire forest and desert beyond. Pursing for breath Faith could hear the heavy footsteps and breathing of Chancellor Becket a long way below her, and the faint voice of encouragement from the young Fairy whom Berberdoff had sent with the message.

"Not far now," Faith muttered to herself as she made a great effort up the last few steps.

Suddenly she burst through the door at the top of the stairwell. Bright sunlight greeted her. Blinking, she tried to clear her eyes.

"Welcome Royal Princess, I hope the climb was not too tiring. But I thought you would want to see this for yourself." Faith heard Berberdoff say a little way off to her side.

Opening her eyes after the dark, she looked around. As a child she had spent many hours up in the watch tower, gazing across the horizon, dreaming of far off lands and adventure. The view as always took her breath away. A thick canopy of tree top leaves lay out in front of her like a crumpled blanket. The occasional brightly coloured bird burst out of the canopy, only to quickly plunge back down.

"It's beautiful," Faith said almost to herself. A cough bought her back to Berberdoff who was looking at her with a questioning expression on his face.

"It is indeed a spectacular view, Royal Princess," Berberdoff said, "only spoilt by that!" He pointed far out towards where the sky meets the horizon. Faith looked to where he had indicated, and then walked the short distance to get a better look.

"This had better be worth all the climbing!" An exhausted, gasping Chancellor Becket spluttered from behind her. Turning to look Faith saw a very red faced Chancellor, sweat streaming down his temples being helped to a seat on the side of the watch tower by the young Fairy messenger.

"It is worth the climb," Berberdoff said from beside Faith, "but I cannot say you will be happy on the long return journey?"

Looking back over the canopy, Faith strained her eyes to see what she was looking for. "I cannot see anything," Faith said.

"Look, just over where the trees end, and before the horizon," Berberdoff said as he pointed out in the direction he was indicating, "A thin black line, it is not much to see from here but that line is the problem!"

"What problem?" Chancellor Becket asked between gasps for breath. Turning around to see Becket Berberdoff, he continued, "They are the Destroyer's creatures. I have sent a few volunteers' to take a closer look. There must be millions of them and they nearly surround the entire Dark Forest!"

"What are they doing here, what do they want?" Faith said, fear breaking though her voice.

"It does not matter what they think they are doing here," Becket replied with confidence, "we are protected by magic, and those creatures will never be able to entire." Faith felt a little better until Berberdoff spoke again.

"That may be so, they cannot gain entry into the Dark Wood. But they are already in the Dark Forest, and that is where we gather our food and other needs."

Berberdoff said, "And Tim, when he was here asked questions about the Destroyer's creatures being helped by magic. Have you found any answers yet?"

Chancellor Becket gave Berberdoff a hard stare before answering. Faith could feel the tension.

"Sir Timothy made several wild allegations, none of which had any grounding in truth. We have looked into what he said but I know we will not find anything as there is nothing to find."

Becket said, "I think we should carry on this conversation back down stairs, where we can look at all our options." Faith said, and without another word made for the door which lead to the stairs and a long trip back down.

The decent was much quicker than the climb. She hurried down as fast as she could, but still feeling safe on the stairs. Far above her she could already hear Berberdoff and Becket, noisily making their way down, arguing as they went. Faith hoped by the time they had reached the ground they would had stopped arguing and began to find some answers.

The two guards at the bottom of the watch tower tree leapt to attention as Faith walked through the door, she hardly noticed them. Walking as quickly as she could along the open wooded corridor she unfolded her wings and unconsciously began to flap them. The breeze was nice and refreshing after the excess of the climb and decent.

She approached the throne room, this also was guarded by two Fairies who saluted in unison as she approached. Nodding in reply she entered thought the door which was opened just before she reached it.

Inside, she headed directly for the long rugged looking table which was positioned to the left of the double thrones. The table was almost the length of the room with ornate chairs on either side. At the head stood a very grand chair, decorated with carvings of different aspects of Fairy life. This was the crown's chair, the one which could only be occupied by the current ruling monarch.

Faith didn't even glance at this spectacular chair as she passed it, making her way to the other end of the table. Here stood an almost as ornate a chair as the one at the head of the table, but smaller in every way. It seemed to be an exact copy of the other chair but on a smaller scale. This is where Faith sat and waited. This was the chair which showed the authority of the Crown Prince of the Dark Forest or, in Faith's case Princess. As Faith sat and waited she reflected on the amount of chairs on each side of the long table. She believed in years long passed this table was the centre of knowledge and wisdom, sort by all types of beings thought out the entire world.

The click of a closing door bought Faith back to the present. Berberdoff and Becket slowly walked along the side of the long table towards her. Their conversation had ceased, Faith hoped this was a sign they had come to some sort of agreement, or at the very least an arrangement.

As they reached the end of the table, Berberdoff and Beckett, each pulled out a chair and sat down, their eyes focused towards her - no one spoke.

"I want a meeting of the Star Chamber called." Faith said breaking the silence. The look of horror on Chancellor Beckets face betrayed his thoughts.

"You cannot do that," he gasped, "the Star Chamber is the privilege of the King. It does not just respond to the summons of anyone!"

"I am the Royal Princess," Faith replied in a voice which would have frozen a lesser man, "I am hardly anyone."

"I know Royal Princess," Becket replied, "and I mean no insult to you. But as you know the Star Chamber only answers to the ruling monarch. They may well just ignore you, which would be very insulting." Silence filled the room as Faith considered her response. She knew Becket was right, which made her that little bit more determined to stick to her request.

"We have the Destroyer's creatures surrounding the Dark Forest. We do not know their intentions or motivation." She raised a hand to cut Becket's question off. "They have not crossed barren desert for days on end for no reason. So why are they here? If that is not a question for the Star Chamber, never mind who askes it I do not know what is."

Chancellor Becket opened his mouth to reply, but then closed it without uttering a sound. He just sat closely examining his fingers, as if he had just noticed them for the first time. It was Berberdoff who was the first to speak.

"I do not know who this Star Chamber is, they do sound important. But I would suggest there is still plenty we can decide and set into motion before and even if they meet and come up with some answers."

"I agree," Becket said, much to Faith's surprise, "we do not know if the Star Chamber will meet, and even if they do why should they have any more knowledge about the creatures than we do? At the moment we are stacking up question upon question. I purpose we try to get some answers before the questions overwhelm us."

Chapter 3

Tagan walked through the wide corridors of the palace towards the War room responding with a smile and nod to all the salutes he received. If he looked happy and confident, the mood would spread. The last thing Tagan would have regarded himself as at the moment was happy or confident. Yes, they had saved Kleve. But at what cost?

The crowded palace corridors were an example of the result. Still after weeks the palace accommodated a great deal of the misplaced and refugee population of Kleve and the surrounding country side. A great many had returned to try and recover their lives. But building work was slow, and a large proportion still did not believe the danger had passed.

Arriving at the imposing door of the War room Tagan hesitated, this was the sixth day of talking about the way forward with no clear plan emerging.

"If you have a moment, Your Royal Highness?" A calm silk like voice said from behind Tagan. Turning, he almost jumped as he looked up at the impressive but unnerving figure of Stickleback the leader of The Guardian, and standing beside him Major Lord Bazzington. Although The Guardian who followed The Champion Lord was very much a part of the fight against the Destroyer, and had played a critical part in the victory at Kleve, seeing one standing inside a corridor of the palace was slightly unnerving. "I am sorry if I alarmed you."

"No, no," Tagan replied as he regained his composure, "I was in a world of my own. How can I help you?"

"You have already helped us and that is what I was about to thank you for." Stickleback said. Tagan still did not know what he was being thanked for, and this must have shown by the confused look which prompted Lord Bazzington to say:

"I think my Lord, what my friend is thanking you for is the land you have granted to us. We have begun to construct a barracks and a village on the area of Frankwell." Stickleback nodded in response.

"Frankwell," Tagan replied, "the other side of the river, it is known to flood regularly and is marsh land. That is not suitable at all, come and sees me after the meeting and I will get it changed. I will not have supporters of Mercia given short change."

"But Your Highness," Stickleback said, "the area is most suitable, and we were told about the flooding and marsh. We have taken this into account."

"My Lord, the Guardian are very industrial builders and have made great improvements. They are also helping a great deal in the reconstruction of Kleve. You would be impressed."

Looking at both of them standing in front of him, a large insect and a human he could hear the pride in their voices.

"I am sure I would and will be. After this meeting I would like to see what you have done, if that would be alright?"

"It would be an honour my Lord." Stickleback said.

Turning back towards the door Tagan entered the War room. It was a hive of activity with most of the people who Tagan would have expected to see there. But as Tagan scanned the room there seemed to be one obvious omission.

"The Champion Lord has still not returned yet?" he asked.

"We are expecting him any moment now, Your Highness." Stickleback answered. Tim, the Champion Lord had left several days ago to gain more information about the Destroyer's creatures, how he was doing this Tagan had not asked and Tim was not forthcoming. But until he returned they had very little to go on.

Bang, bang, bang, the room was called to order by Lord Avon and everyone gained their seats, sitting beside Lord Avon was Prince Sebastian, the Queen's husband and Tagan's brother-in-law. Tagan sat in the front row with Field Marshal Sylvester Hungerford, or plane Sylvester as he preferred to be called, on one side and General Lord Cogan on the other, beside him Mortimer, although he had no military knowledge Tagan had asked him for his experience and the fact he had been involved from the beginning. Behind his in order of rank sat the rest of his officers of the Allied Army. Marine General Butterworth, General Sidney Goberton, Commandant Stockton with all their aides and advisors. A short distance away Tagan could see Stickleback and Lord Bazzington with their offices from The Guardian and close to them several Griffins. The rest of the room was made up of Commanders of the Mercian army.

"May I have your attention please so we can make a start," Lord Avon, the Commander of all Mercian Forces said, "I hope that The Champion Lord will be joining us soon with his latest report on the Destroyer's Army, maybe I'll even be interrupted." He then went on to outline all the known facts, a groan from the audience indicated they had already been told this many times before.

"I'm sorry we are late and apologise for interrupting." Tim's voice broke through the opening door to the War room. All heads turned as if in unison to see The Champion Lord. He looked tired with dust covered cloths which gave the impression of being slept in for days on end.

Megan stood on one side of him, Titus another Fairy the other, just behind them appeared in the doorway some of the Guardian, members of Tim's personal escort, the Flying Wildbloods. Faith looked as stunning as she always did, not a hair out of place, her cloths clean and tidy, this was no accident Tagan thought, keeping an appearance to such a high standard took a great deal of effort, and from the short time he had got to know Megan he believed all the effort would be hers. Titus' cloths had the appearance of hard wearing, but not as worn out as Tim's cloths.

"You are most welcome my Lord Champion," Lord Avon said, "and I believe we are all eager to hear your report." Tim smiled with a nod in response.

"Before I start, Lord Avon, could you please give me the answer to the question I asked via my messenger?"

"Yes, of course," Lord Avon said, "your question was, just so everyone in the room knows, how many of the Destroyer's creatures still remain at large throughout the countries? Well using several Griffins to fly to several countries which we knew were having defectives, the answer has come back, none, we can find no trace of any of the creatures." A general murmur of approval spread around the room on hearing the news.

"That is very good news, and better than I had expected." Tim replied. Titus and two of the Guardian who had entered the War room had taken seats, but Megan stood solidly by Tim's side. "I think I can say with confidence with this information and from our observation, that all the Destroyer's creatures are now surrounding the Dark Forest."

"Good news?" Avon asked, "I believe it is good for all the countries that have been blighted by these creatures. But how will it help us if we intend to destroy them?" A murmur again went around the room, hushed only when Prince Sebastian rose to his feet to speak.

"I have said before, you know, um Lord Champion," the Price began, "we should now just leave these evil creatures to rot in the baking sun of the desert, I would not risk a man's life trying to chase after them." A few claps and noises of encouragement punctuated his words. "If they return we wait and strike at them at the point they cross out of the desert, a place where we can be ready, on our terms and on our ground." Cheers and clapping filled the room as nearly the entire audience rose to its feet at once. The only exception was Tagan, his most senior officers and the Guardian.

Tim smiled as he watched the reaction, Prince Sebastian acknowledged the cheers as he sat down satisfied with his work and confident his plan would be enacted. Turning to Stickleback Tim said something which was hid in the general commotion, he was handed one of the golden arrows which were recovered after the battle of Mountain hold, an arrow which had killed Aaron the last known Golden Griffin.

Tim held the arrow in his hands, inspecting it intensely, as the room came to order he held it up in his left hand not high but so everyone could see it.

"This is the type of arrow which killed my brother Aaron. He was the last living Golden Griffin so far as we know. He was also the greatest threat to the Destroyer and its creatures. How that threat was to be enacted we will never know, Aaron was killed before his full potential was reached. But the Destroyer knew, and acted to stop him. I give you the golden arrow." The room was hushed as Tim spoke.

"I know some of you have seen these arrows, some even keep them as a mark of rank. But have any of you looked at them, no, I mean really looked at them?" From the intense silence Tim knew he now had the full attention of the room, now he needed to take them on a journey of no return. "This arrow is made from pure gold, no other trace elements to strengthen it, just pure gold. I know - I have had a gold smith melt one down to see what else was in it, nothing just pure gold. Look at the arrow head, it is sharp, sharper than most arrow heads made by the best armours, and it is made for one task and one task only, to kill a Golden Griffin, the tip is sharp in order to pierce flesh deep into the body, and then these hooks," Tim pointed to some very sharp rear facing hooks on each side of the arrow head, "these are to stop the arrow being pulled out without a great deal of damage to the inner organs. The shaft, look at it strait and strong, a perfect balanced arrow which will follow a true course, and the tail feathers. This is the best craftsmanship I have ever seen. Each feather is perfect, as if it had just been plucked from a bird. But they have not!" Tim's voice rose with each part of the explanation, he was not shouting, but each word was emphasised in his strong voice.

"What has made this arrow and all the other golden arrows is magic." An audible intake of breath, followed by stunned silence. "No master craftsman has ever laid hands on this weapon. I have asked some of the best in the world to copy it and all have failed. Gold is too soft to have a shaft this thin and still be strong enough to be shot from a bow and strike and kill a target. Once you have fathomed that concept the whole of the rest of the arrow falls to pieces, the arrow head and especially the tail feathers. The only way this could have been made is with the use of magic." Silence filled the room. Tim sat down with Megan who patted his hand and whispered something into his ear. No one spoke or moved, all deep in their thoughts.

Tagan was the first to stand up, He knew what Tim had said made perfect sense, but he also believed Tim had not finished telling them all of his argument. Tagan believed he knew what Tim would say, and would try to help him.

"Thank you Lord Champion for your explanation, and I cannot argue with any of your logic. But the question I have for you is why we cannot just stay here as Prince Sebastian has suggested and wait for the creatures to return?"

"The answer is simple," Tim replied without standing again, "If we wait we will all die." Tagan was a bit surprised at the bluntness of the answer, but before he could ask another question of Tim, Tim stood up.

"You see, with every encounter won or lost the creatures have adapted. When we first met them they could only use their claws, sharp as they are to fight. In a short time they have found the knowhow and capability to use weapons, bows and arrows to just mention two. They are now able to fly. If this was natural it would take many life times for them to adapt, not a few years like they are doing. My army The Guardian are a response to these creatures which they call the plague. The Creator has put in place a safe guard against any one type of creature overrunning the rest. But this is different, this time they are larger, stronger and can adapt quickly to a changing situation. I believe, as you yourself my Lord have been told, they do not originate through natural breading."

Tagan had to nod his head to that, he was also present when they were told about the caves of cocoons' having captured humans being put into and fully grown creatures emerging.

"The only place in the world where magic this powerful is known is the Dark Forest. I suggest the creatures know this and are only there for one of two reasons. First they are there to take and use the magic, or second, which I hope to be wrong, they are being directed from the Dark Forest!" Silence filled the room as Tim's words faded, this time he did sit down.

It was some time before Prince Sebastian stood again, this time he did not need to wait for quiet, everyone seemed caught up in their own private thoughts.

"I am willing to admit when I am wrong, and in this case I believe I am. So with the authority of the Queen, and I must say after discussing it with Lord Avon I am transferring two Mercian Armies to the Allied Army with immediate effect. Also Lord Trentham, the head of our Diplomatic Corps has been hard at work and by the end of the week we believe you will have armies or parts of them from most countries, all in support of you and willing to cross the desert to fight the Destroyer's creatures. " This was followed by quite a lot of clapping and even some cheers, this however, stopped as Field Marshal Roderick Sylvester Hungerford rose to his feet, although the smallest person in the room, he seemed to fill it with his authoritarian presence.

"Thank you Your Highness for this most generous offer of support, but I must decline most of what you have said," Sylvester said, slowly walking from his seat to a more central place in the room where he could see everyone, and everyone was hanging on his every word, apart from Lord Cogan, who seemed to be taking notes, "What we need now more than ever is a direction to be heading in, and a well set out Command team. I will now give you both!"

"All our forces which are to seek out the creatures will come under the overall command of Prince Tagan, as I would hope you all would agree." He stopped to look around the room, but did not ask for agreement or approval. "I will command the Allied Army and the Champion Lord the Guardian of course," Sylvester nodded towards Tim who nodded back in acknowledgement, "the two armies which you offer us again I thank you, but we will take only one, the reformed Royal Southern Army, and they will be under the command of General Lord Cogan," he lifted a hand to stop any questions before they could start, "and we will not be taking any of the well-meaning armies from any other countries, I now believe some of you may have some questions?"

To begin with no one spoke, as if shocked into silence, then Lord Avon, a world renowned military genius cleared his throat,

"I can see the logic in you appointing Lord Cogan, and fully approve of that, but if what the Champion Lord has told us, and I am not disputing him at all, why are you turning down more troops to help you?"

"A very good question and one which has vexed me for some time, you see I thought when the creatures left our lands a lot of people would, thinking we had won, would offer us help. Well we haven't won, far from it, we could even be on the edge of losing in a very big way, and that is why we must turn them down. I will explain."

"We are about to launch the largest army into a hostile land with no way of supporting ourselves, we must take everything we need to survive, food, water, weapons everything. For every fighting soldier we will need about six supporting soldier. On top of that it is my honest belief, and in this I agree with the Champion Lord, that the creatures have left and gone in to the desert as a trap for us!"

"If you think you're going into a trap, Field Marshal," Prince Sebastian asked, "Why not find another way?"

"Because, as the Champion Lord has already said, the creatures are adapting all the time. We have to go to them and try to destroy them, or as many as possible before we all get killed, if that happens, which I must say is a very likely outcome, at least you would have assembled a large army here to fight and hopefully destroy what remains of the creatures!" Sylvester said before finally sitting down. Muttering filled the room until Lord Avon gained silence with a few hard bangs on the table.

"Field Marshal, I can agree with all that you have said, so I have one simple question, when do you intend to leave?"

"Not for a few months yet, we have a lot to do before we leave, and I also want the winter weather to start in the desert, that way we will not have to fight the full heat as well."

"But what will you do in the mean time?" Avon asked.

"I do not really think we will have the luxury of time which you think, Lord Avon, once we start our preparations in full." Lord Cogan said for the first time.

"Very well," Prince Sebastian said as he rose to his feet, "you have our full support and Lord Avon will give you any supplies you need. I think we will close this meeting now and arrange to meet again in about two weeks to check on progress. All agreed?" A murmur of approval filled the room as the officers began to talk about what they had heard, and lined up to get orders from the Field Marshal and Lord Cogan, who seemed to already be in the know.

Tagan sat and watched the milling Generals, they all seemed happy with their orders as they received them, with a few shocked faces. Then the main door was opened and the leaders of the supporting staff entered, although they worked with the army all the time, this was probably the first time they had been bought into a briefing. As the room emptied until only Tagan, Tim, with Megan sitting beside him of course, and Stickleback with Lord Bazzington looking on with intense interest, then Cogan and Sylvester remained with the twenty or so leaders of the support staff.

Cogan spoke, "Gentlemen, you and your men are the key to this whole battle, we will have to take everything we need to live, food, water, for both men and animals, for the fighting soldiers and for your own soldiers. On top of that, the further we get into the desert, the longer that supply chain will be, and I can guarantee the creatures will attack it, you are both the most important life line and our weakest link, and at the moment I haven't got the soldiers to help protect you!"

Tagan would have thought the support staff leaders would have become alarmed at this, but not a bit of it, they just seemed to accept it and nod their heads.

"So how are you going to be protected? All of your men, whatever their jobs will be equipped with appropriate weapons, be it short swords, bows or staffs, and trained in how to use them to protect themselves." This seemed to go down with general approval.

"On top of this we will lay a railway of wooden rails across the desert and adapt the carts to run on them, this way each horse or mule will be able to pull a heavier load quicker, this railway must be protected, or repaired very quickly if damaged." Again approval, "And last of all, you will be given army ranks to fit a person with your responsibility, this will also be filtered down to your men so you have a command stricter, do any of you have any questions?"

Tagan turned to Tim as the questions were asked, "Why didn't I think of that? It's so simple and I think it will work very well."

"Sylvester is something of a military genius I think," Tim replied with a smile on his face.

Chapter 4

"I am sorry Royal Princess, but that is their final word." Chancellor Beckett said in a low, down cast voice. The news he had bought to Faith was not what she had expected or indeed wanted. The Star Chamber had refused to meet and discuss the problem of the creatures surrounding the Dark Forest. They did not see it as a problem to trouble them and Faith was not the King, just the Royal Princess and therefore could not compel them to talk about it.

"Well I see it as a problem, a very big problem which we will just have to deal with ourselves!" Faith said in a louder voice than she had intended. Along the large table in the throne room apart from herself sat Chancellor Beckett and Berberdoff.

"I totally agree with you, Royal Princess," Beckett said, "how do you suggest we start dealing with this problem?"

"We stop talking and start acting!" Berberdoff said banging his fists in the oak table top to emphasise his words. "We have been surrounded for over a week now, and apart from us three talking, nothing has been done. I say before we leave here today we have a plan which can be put immediately into action so our people can see we are acting and let them believe we know what we are doing." He sat back, his fiery eyes glaring a challenge towards Faith, and especially Beckett.

Faith sat in silence contemplating her options. She knew she must act, indecision was dangerous but an overreaction could be just as bad. But Berberdoff was right, her people needed to be doing something to show she had control of the situation.

"Right, I want the Guard expanded from the few hundred which we have now to five thousand. I know that will not be anywhere close to the numbers we will require if we do have to fight, but it will be a good start. The Dark Forest will have its own army!" Berberdoff's eyes lit up as Faith spoke. Beckett looked stunned, as if all meaning had just left his world.

"Royal Princess," Beckett began to plead his case, "We are a peaceful people we know nothing of fighting. You cannot honestly believe we could fight the numbers of creatures surrounding the Dark Forest and win?"

"Correct, I do not believe we can fight them and win." Faith said in reply, "But we are going to take an active role in our destiny. Right Chancellor Beckett, please go and find me the Commander of the Guard, he has a promotion coming."

"Do you think that is wise?" Berberdoff asked. "I know Commander Avtag is a good man, and of course your cousin Royal Princess, but placing him in charge of an army?"

"He will not be in charge of the army, I will. I am making myself the Forest Marshal, the head of the Army of the Dark Forest. Avtag I will make a General, he will be in overall operational command." Faith said, receiving nods of approval from both Beckett and Berberdoff.

But before Beckett raised to leave, Berberdoff had one last question. "I totally agree with what you are trying to do, but Chancellor Beckett has a good point, we cannot defeat the creatures. What is the other part of your plan?"

Faith smiled at the question. Now she knew at least one of her advisers was beginning to think positively. "I want you to find three of the fittest Fairies we have. Their job is to fly and find the army which I know Prince Tagan will be leading to help us. They must not only get to that army but must get back to tell us they are coming. It will be dangerous, but at least one of them must make it back to us."

"I will find the best three men I have." Berberdoff said as he stood up.

"No!" Beckett said bringing silence to the room. "We will need every able bodied man wc have here to, if necessary fight. I know what you are trying to do and I agree, but I would suggest sending female Fairies. They are lighter, can fly just as fast, and possibly longer. It is as you say dangerous as you say, but I think three female Fairies would have just as good a chance, if not better." Berberdoff stopped standing and just looked at Beckett. Then slowly nodding he said.

"Yes, I can see your logic. Three women it will be then, I will get them now."

Both men rose and left to undertake their separate tasks leaving Faith alone in the large throne room. She smiled, at last she thought I am taking charge, I am leading my people. She felt a great feeling of satisfaction.

*****

The overhanging trees gave shade to the open forest floor. This was also the gathering place for Fairies to try out their wings. Dozens of fairies from both clans twisted and turned in the confined airspace just below the forest canopy. The potential for collisions was high, and a small gathering of injured Fairies laid witness to this.

Since the clan Fairies had arrived and discovered they could in fact now fly, the training ground had been packed from dawn to dust, by Fairies from the Dark Forest trying to help and encourage their long lost cousins in the art of flying. The biggest challenge to the clan Fairies was take off. Unlike their Dark Forest cousins who could just take to the air from a standing position, they being on the most part slightly bigger framed, with heavier wings, required a running take off. Normally this would be no problem. But now as the forest was surrounded, it had become one.

Starlight looked upon the scene of twisting bodies in the undignified aerial dance of the competing Fairies to become airborne.

"Are you too accompanied to now be involved?" A voice asked from behind her. Starlight did not look around to see who was speaking, she recognised the voice of Dew, a very slim and petite Fairy from the Dark Forest who had been helping her to master the art of flying.

"No, you know I'm not," Starlight replied, "but trying to fly here is too dangerous and too tiring. I flap like mad to get up, only to have to land a moment later. There must be a better way?"

"Well I do have an idea which may help." Dew said drawing up beside her to watch the chaos unfold in front of them. "I was talking to some of the Elders, they think, or some of them do, that your wings are designed for souring on thermals. Not for flapping like ours."

Starlight looked at her, she did not understand what she was being told, but would give anything a try once.

"We need to get above the tree canopy to find out." Dew said. Now that was something Starlight was more than willing to try. Scrambling down from their view point the pair of Fairies made their way to the forest floor.

"Where are you two going with such a determined look on your faces?" Windfall, another of the clan Fairies said, her face glowing from the beads of sweat running down her face from the physical effort of flying.

"To above the tree canopy," Starlight replied without breaking step. She then realised Windfall, without a word had joined them. Dew looked at her but said nothing. At the far end of the clearing Dew stopped and turned around, looking at the other two she said.

"Take off and flap hard, you must climb as fast as you can and aim for that gap in the tree canopy," she pointed to the spot with an outstretched arm, "it is larger than it looks from here, I will follow you up."

Without another word Starlight opened her wings and gave them a few hard flaps. Then she began to run as fast as she could, her wings beating up and down. Soon her feet were as light as a feather as she took to the air. Beating her wings with as much power as she could muster, she rose faster and faster. Aiming for the gap in the overhanging canopy, she burst through, as if gaining air from the surface of water.

A few hard flaps on her wings shot her above the green canopy. Starlight looked around an ore. Above her shone a blazing sun in a deep blue sky, only the odd cloud breaking the clear air. Far above her shored large birds, Vultures she thought with their effortless flight, gliding in the thermals. Gaining height she edged towards the limit of the Dark Forest, here the air seemed warmer and a lot dryer.

Suddenly Starlight shot up, rapidly gaining height, she immediately knew she had entered a thermal, a column of hot rising air. Without thinking she began to circle, the way she had seen Vultures flying.

A chill in the air broke her concentration, looking down she shuddered. Far, far below was the deep green canopy of the Dark Forest, the trees merged into each other giving the impression of an impenetrable barrier of vegetation in the middle of the endless desert!

Then it struck her, from this height she could see could see the entire Dark Forest, looking a little further she saw a dark moving mass, individuals did not stick out unless they were alone, but the general movement in an unorganized swirl told her those were the creatures. From this height Starlight could see that the creatures did indeed surround the Dark Forest, but in some places with very few creatures, but in others they were massed. But she could see no order to them.

As she flew from one thermal to another, losing a little height in between, but rapidly gaining it again as she circled inside the rising column of air she noticed she had flown quite far out into the desert. A slight feeling of panic overcame her as she realised this, and the fact she had also flown further than the outermost circle of creatures which surrounded the Dark Forest, the panic was reinforced when she saw about ten flying creatures flying up towards her.

Tilting her wings she hoped she would reach the perceived safety of the Dark Forest before they reached her, because if she did not she could not imagine what she would do.

Diving towards a thermal, gaining height and quickly diving to the next she looked down in a frightful state, she had taken her eyes off the creatures and now was quickly trying to locate them, which was not an easy task.

But then she saw them and was surprised to see they were still far below, slowly she glided in an effortless wide circle watching them, her breathing was deep but slow, and it just seemed natural. As she flew she realised that the creatures, never mind how hard they seemed to try could not gain the height to get any were near to her height, they seemed to be struggling up a short way and then falling back quite a height.

With a smile on her face a small chuckle in her throat, and a lot more confidence, she headed back towards the centre of the canopy of the Dark Forest.

Below movement dew her eyes, far, far below she saw the slow determine flapping of Windfall as she tried to gain height, suddenly she shot up at the same time as her wings Dew still far below and looking as she would not gain any height.

Starlight flew in wide effortless circles waiting for Windfall to join her at her altitude.

"What do you think?" she asked as Windfall joined her in the relaxed circle,

"This is fantastic," Windfall replied, pure joy filling her voice, "I can see forever, and isn't the Dark Forest small from here?"

They stayed slowly flying from thermal to thermal, relaxed and using no effort, until Starlight noticed the shadow of the Dark Forest lengthening.

"I think we should go back down, it will be dark soon and I haven't seen Dew in a while," Starlight said. Together the two Fairies lost height over the tree canopy looking for the gap from which they had escaped.

"Look!" Shouted Windfall pointing ahead to show Starlight, on the top of a large tree watching them approach, sat Dew, a wide smile spread across her face. As they approached she took off and then guided them throw the gap and down to the forest floor.

Not a moment too soon Starlight thought as she looked around at the gloom of the inner canopy, as all three alighted Dew was the first to speak, her enthusiasm unbounded.

"You flew so high, and it looked so effortless, what was it like being so high?"

"I don't really know," Windfall replied, "it just seemed so natural."

The three Fairies talked excitedly as they walked to the main tree house, the rest of the forest was now empty, other Fairies choosing company and security now darkness was drawing in.

The bright lights on entry to the hall were a contrast to the gathering gloom of outside, but not as noticeable as the sudden silence which abruptly fell as their arrival was noticed. Standing still all three Fairies wore expressions of worry and concern.

Two older members of the Guard approached them,

"Are you the two who flew out from the cover of the Dark Forest?" The taller guard asked, timidly Starlight and Windfall nodded, "Well you had better come with us, you to please," he said, adding a nod towards Dew.

The three of them followed the two guards along familiar corridors to Dew, but Starlight and Windfall looked around in awe at the woodworking ability of the Dark Forest Fairies.

Soon they came to a place which both clan Fairies recognised, the main doors to the grand chamber, Starlight had a sickening feeling in the pit of her stomach. This was the place where they had all first been welcomed, if they were taken in there she knew they were in deep trouble.

But they passed without a pause, turning into a much narrower corridor with doors spaced out equally on each side, Starlight thought they must be some type of offices or bed chambers, there was so many and in a uniformed order. About a third of the way the two guards stopped outside one of the doors, it looked no different to any of the others which they had passed, but this was where their fate would be decided.

Knocking on the dark wooden door the guard disappeared inside without a word, leaving the other guard outside with Starlight and the other two Fairies. No one spoke, all caught up in their own thoughts.

"THEY DID WHAT!" A load voice shouted from behind the partly open door, "HOW HIGH?" It asked, but Starlight could not hear the answer, now she did feel sick!

The door suddenly swung fully open and the guard who was inside beckoned the three girls in, the other guard stayed outside.

"Go and tell Berberdoff I need to see him immediately, do you know which room he is in?" The older, Fairy asked, his voice and bearing held the manner of authority. Starlight was worried, when the guard was told to fetch Berberdoff, the leader of their clan, but seeing the totally drained expression on Dew's face!

As they waited, standing in the middle of the room in front of a large wooden table, which the older male Fairy sat behind, Starlight tried to look around the room, without being obvious.

Behind the desk and chair was a book case from floor to ceiling and the entire length of the wall, Starlight thought she had never seen so many book and scrolls in one place outside a library before. Behind where they were standing were several high backed chairs, which they were not offered, and to the back of the room several more comfy chairs and two settees.

The door opened without notice and in strolled Berberdoff, his expression was unreadable as he took all three girls in with a long steady look.

To the guard who was hovering at the door the old man behind the desk said,

"Thank you, that will be all," as the door closed behind the guard, he looked at Berberdoff and said, "From what I have been informed, the two from your clan are the main two culprits, if you want to call it that."

"Yes, I have just been told the same by your, messenger," Berberdoff said as he walked into the centre of the room and took a seat in one of the high backed chairs just to their side and behind them, "just how high did you get?" he asked.

The three girls looked at each other, Starlight knew she must have done wrong and she had encouraged Windfall, but

Dew stayed behind, so she knew she must take the blame and any punishment.

"Well, Sir, I'm sorry but," she began, but was cut off by Dew.

"No, it was my fault. I should have not encouraged them." She suddenly stopped as the older man stood up and walked from behind the table.

"I think you should all take a seat, and tell us exactly what happened, take your time, but we want to know every last detail." He said taking a chair opposite Berberdoff.

The three girls each took a seat behind them and between Berberdoff and who Dew whispered to Windfall and Starlight was Chancellor Becket. They then, in as much detail as they could recall began to relay their flying that day, how Starlight had been able to use thermals to gain height with no real effort and before she knew it was able to see the whole Dark Forest and the creatures beyond, and how she had, without realising flown out into the desert, then seen the flying creatures flying towards her, but not being able reach her height. Then she and Windfall had flown within the boundary of the Dark Forest to quite a height, until they could see the shadows lengthening so they returned and found Dew sitting on a tree on the top of the canopy.

"Why did you not go and join them?" Chancellor Becket asked Dew when the girls had finished their explanation.

"I tried to, but I could not gain the height, I got so far up but never mind what I did, I could not gain any more height." Dew said.

The two men looked at each other in the silence which followed a slight smile on Berberdoff's face, which he was trying to hide, but just concern from Becket. The three girls said nothing looking from one man to another, nervously awaiting their fate.

It was Berberdoff who spoke first. "Well, Chancellor, I think we have found our volunteers, but I am rather concerned with Dew." Dew looked alarmed at the statement.

"I agree," Becket said, "but I rather think we should explain what we want and let her decide?"

"Very well," Berberdoff began to explain, "As you know, and have seen we are surrounded by creatures, these same creatures have been roaming the human world and destroying everything in their path. Prince Tagan and others have been battling these creatures. Now we want you three to fly to Kleve where we believe Prince Tagan is with his army and ask him for help, in our view it will be better to take steps to defend ourselves than to wait to see what the creatures' intentions are." The three girls' faces were full of smiles with every word they heard, Becket's showed more concern.

"But, I must stress," He said, "this is not a one way trip, we want you to return with an answer, so we know what his intentions are!"

"Well I think Windfall and I could fly there and back with little trouble, but I'm sorry to say Dew may have some problems on the return trip, the creatures may well be waiting for us and she cannot fly over them." Starlight said after a few moments to think.

"That is what I'm afraid of." Becket said as Dew announced,

"If you two are going I'm not going to be left behind."

"Good," Berberdoff said, "I hoped you would say that, because the last time I spoke to Prince Tagan I gave him the impression that the Dark Forest Fairies should not be trusted. I hope with you with Starlight and Windfall it will show a united front to him."

"But what of the problem that creatures are ready for them on their return journey, which Starlight has already pointed out?" Becket asked

"I will be alright, I am not being left behind!" Dew said in a firm voice, just as Starlight was saying.

"I did not mean to say Dew should not come, it was just something we would have to overcome."

"I agree, it is a problem which we will have to look into, and I will give it a great deal of thought," Berberdoff said, "but I think we have made enough decisions. Over the next two days I want you to plan your flights, how you intend to get over the creatures without being seen, Dew, and Windfall and Starlight, I want you two to become more practiced flyers and to find out what dangers lay out beyond the creatures?"

With very little more fuss, the three Fairies left the office to make their way back to their own rooms. The guards must have left some time ago. They all felt very excited at the prospect of such an adventure, but had been cautioned not to reveal anything to anyone, which made it that little bit more exciting!

Chapter 5

"I just don't understand it?" Said Colonel Peabody as he read the early morning reconnaissance reports laid out on the small table in front of him. "I can see no sign of anything of the creatures. They just seem to have disappeared!"

"Well the reports don't lie," Said Erwin, who had also been reading them, "What the Field Marshall put in his letter to you about the creatures leaving Kleve must have been a catalyst for them leaving everywhere."

"Well, are we ready to march?" Peabody asked no one in particular and was given the answer,

"Yes."

"Well, let's get going." He ordered. Turning to Erwin and Major Gladstone who had also be reading the reports, "We are about two days march from Kleve, if we push it we can make that a day and a half, that will mean we should arrive at Kleve at about the same time as the Greater Longman's Army."

Bugle calls filled the early morning as the march was announced, very shortly the front ranks began to move forward, Soldiers of both sexes closer to the rear of the column hurriedly broke down the very last tents and along with the tables stacked them onto a waiting cart.

Peabody stood and watched his army slowly pass by, all the mounted units lead their horses on foot, there is no point riding horses if they outpaced the infantry, and now they had quite a large infantry made up of archers and pike men, which was ironic as most of them were women. But just as aggressive and determined as their male colleagues.

At the rear came the baggage train, this was made up of horse drawn carts and included all the supplies, tenting, the cooks and medical staff and the wounded, of which there were still quite a few. The skirmishes which had given birth to this very unique army had been very violent and very bloody, the men and especially the women had earned the right to march in this army, which was one of the reasons the Greater Longman's Army were accompanying them to Kleve.

Mounting his horse Peabody rode, along with Gladstone and Erwin, to the front of the army, here he dismounted and leading his horse, walked along side Willow. She was older than Peabody by quite a few years, but she had a very youthful appearance with a very sharp and active mind, which fooled people to thinking she was younger than she was. This was also the main reason why she had been head of the village women's council and had been looking after the village, whose male folk had all been killed. It was the council's idea to ask to join the army and fight the creatures.

"If you would prefer I will get you a horse?" Peabody asked Willow again, it was the same question which he asked her the start of every mornings march, and he already knew the answer.

She looked at him, this morning she had a look in her eyes which he had not noticed before.

"Very well I will ride today." She replied, and before he knew it she had mounted his horse and he was leading her. "Are you happy now?" Peabody was left speechless, not helped by the expression on Gladstone's face as he tried to suppress his laughter. Erwin looked as dispassionate as ever, nothing ever seemed to make him laugh or upset him, Peabody thought, but he was an excellent interpreter of intelligence.

"Two riders approaching at speed!" A report was relayed from the front. Peabody watched as one peeled away in his direction, the other rider Peabody knew would continue towards General Flintlock the commander of the Greater Longmans Army. As the rider drew near, a slight look of confusion flicked across his face as he saw Willow riding the Colonel's horse, a quick scan and he saw Peabody on foot leading it.

Without a moment's hesitation the rider dismounted, saluted Peabody and began to relay his report.

"Sir, we have found a dozen or so caves, at the entrance there are parts of carcasses of both animal and human, it looks like they have been eaten!" he said. Peabody stopped, his full attention on every word of the report, "but it's further into the caves that it really gets strange." The scout hesitated, with a glance at Willow mounted on the horse and fully aware he was the centre of everyone's attention.

"Go on," Peabody encouraged.

"We have found what appear to be cocoons - some open and empty, but others Sir, others seem to still have creatures inside them. I don't know if the creatures inside are dead or alive, but there are several of them!"

"When you say several," Erwin butted in, as was his manner when he did not get the questions answered which he was already thinking of, "exactly how many are you talking about, two, five, ten, twenty, one hundred - how many are several?"

"Well Sir," the scout began, looking between Peabody and Erwin as if unsure who he should now be giving his report to, "I have seen at least ten unopened, but I know others had found more, but we thought we should get the reports back as soon as we could first."

"You did the right thing," Peabody said, before Erwin could respond, then turning to Gladstone, but before he could give an order Gladstone was already in full flow, yelling commands to officers and men. Seeing the activity and having confidence in what Gladstone was doing, Peabody turned to Willow.

"Do you want to come with us, or do you want to stay with the army?"

"I think I will stay here, and yes before you ask you can have your horse back, thank you," Willow said, and with a forced smile she slid form the horse's back. Peabody took full control of his horse as he mounted. He looked down quickly at Willow, but then his concentration was back to the scout.

"Whenever you are ready lead on," Peabody said. The scout, who had also remounted his horse, kicked his stirrups into its sides and turned into his direction of travel. Peabody urged his horse forward as he heard the thumping hooves of his escort joining them. A young lieutenant of the Mounted Marines, whose name did not immediately spring into Peabody's head, galloped alongside him.

"I have a combination of twenty Marines and Lancers Sir, I hope that will be acceptable?!" The Lieutenant shouted across to Peabody above the drumming of the hooves.

The small force soon crossed open grass lands, perfect country for cavalry but their progress slowed as they entered thick woodland. Tall heavy trees and thick undergrowth slowed progress. The scouts must have made a thorough search of the areas through which they were passing.

Peabody saw first one or two of the scouts slightly hidden in the trees, guarding their location. They did not react as Peabody and his party rode in, but their faces looked hollow and grey. Closer at what was a dark gaping hole in the side of a small cliff stood more scouts, but this time they were not guarding. Several seemed to be comforting others who appeared to be vomiting, Peabody noted that as many male as female scouts appeared sick. He felt butterflies in his stomach in anticipation!

Dismounting at the cave entrance, the first impression that struck him was the putrid smell of decay. A young woman who he did not know, but who wore the rank of a Captain of the scouts approached him.

"Sir I'm Captain Summerbee, It was my patrols who discovered the cave."

"Very good Captain, your scouts have done well," Peabody replied, "can you show me what you have found."

With no more fuss the Captain turned around and walked into the darkness of the cave where they saw a group of scouts, these all had cloths tied over their noses and mouths, Peabody and the Captain were each offered one.

Holding the cloth over his mouth and nose he smelt the momentary refreshing smell of lavender.

"As we go further into the cave, you will need the cloth," Captain Summerbee said in a muffled voice. With another escort of four, all holding burning torches to give light, Peabody followed as they moved into the depths.

Beside each gruesome discovery stood one or two scouts, illuminating the scene with torches. To start with Peabody saw open, empty cocoons, hundreds of them, scattered all over the cave floor, cavern after cavern were full of them, occasionally the discarded limbs of animals, and occasionally humans were also on the floor. Captain Summerbee explained that they assumed the remains were the first meals eaten by the creatures as they hatched.

Peabody, standing in the middle of several hundred hatched cocoons, thought about what he had seen. It was bad and the smell putrid, but no worse than any of his troops would have experienced in battle.

With a final scan around the cave, Captain Summerbee began to lead the way further into the cave. Following, Peabody noticed the colours of ore reflecting the light from the flaming torches, the contrast of the beautiful sparkles of light and the horror of what he was there to witness were not lost on him.

Suddenly, Captain Summerbee stopped, the flickering light highlighting the strain written across her face. Peabody knew they had reached the area of what he was here to witness.

"If you have already seen what is in there, I have no problems of going on alone," Peabody said.

"No Sir," Summerbee replied, "we will accompany you - no one deserves to see this alone. But I must warn you that what you see you will never be able to forget. If you wish I could explain what is in the next cave, you would still have all the information you need?"

"Thank you for your concern, but I think I should see with my own eyes what you have discovered." Peabody said. Summerbee nodded her head, then taking a torch from one of their escorts turned to go, Peabody, looking at the expression on the face of the closest scout to him also took his torch, and followed.

The cave they entered was vast and dark, the light from their torches only just illuminated the roof and sides of the cave. There were no scouts holding extra torches for light here.

Looking around Peabody could see cocoons in every different stage of development, most look to still be occupied. But the real horror was the ones which had still only just started, or the process had not properly developed.

These showed what the poor victims were before they developed into creatures.

Peabody suddenly lost control of his stomach, doubling over into uncontrollable convolutions of vomiting!

*****

"Are you alright Sir?" The soft sound of a woman's voice asked, as the warm breeze genteelly caressed his face. Opening his eyes Peabody first noticed sunlight filtering though the tall trees, then looking around him he saw the stern, but concerned face of Captain Summerbee.

"What happened?" Peabody asked as he tried to sit up.

"You were sick and then passed out, Sir," Summerbee replied, "but you are among good company, I can count on less than one hand the people who have not reacted the same way to that part of the cave. I do not know how we will be able to discover the full horror of what that cave holds?"

Slowly getting to his feet Peabody looked around him, he noticed soldiers from the Greater Longmans Army among his own, "Is General Flintlock here?" he asked.

"No Sir," Summerbee replied, "but they also sent people to witness what we have found, Major Arawn has not recovered yet, but I think he should do soon."

"Is Major Gladstone here?" Peabody asked as he stood,

"Yes Sir, both armies have stopped outside the wood, and the Major has sent more troops to guard the cave."

"Good, that is precisely what we must do, and get this information to Kleve as fast as possible," Peabody said, "get me a pen and paper, I want a full report dispatched to Kleve as fast as I can write it!"

As he hurriedly wrote the report, putting in as much detail as he could without feeling nauseous again he felt the presents of someone standing very close to his side, watching his every move. Looking up he saw the worried expression of willow.

"Was it as bad as everyone says?" she asked simply.

"Yes, I'm afraid so, and worse." Peabody replied as he returned to his report.

Peabody slowly became aware of a lot of movement near to the cave entrance, from where he sat he could not see the entrance, for which he was grateful, but it seemed that there was a great many soldiers there. Assuming this was the guard being posted he returned to his report.

"How long do you think it will be before you want us back on the march?" Gladstone asked as he walked up briskly, Peabody looked up at him, just as he dropped hot wax onto the back of the folded report to seal it.

"I take it you have posted and provisioned the guard that we are leaving, so I think we should be moving as soon as we can. Are the Greater Longmans' Army ready to move?" Peabody replied,

"General Flintlock has gone into the cave to have a look for himself, it seems he was not getting anything from the Major who he sent, so he decided to see with his own eyes," Gladstone replied, "but I do not know if he has returned yet."

This was answered as the General quickly walked through the wood from the direction of the cave, several officers and attendants in pursuit, his face looked like thunder!

"I do not believe what I have just seen!" he said in an emotional but hard voice, "Are we ready to move?"

"Yes Sir," Peabody replied, "I have just got to get this dispatch on its way, then we should be moving."

It was a very sombre pair of armies which set foot in the early afternoon, and the mood did not clear that evening or throughout the night. Early the next morning, just after dawn, Peabody walked through the active camp, trying to gauge the mood, talking to different soldiers, listening to their hopes and fears, reassuring them and putting on a braver and more positive face than he felt. As he returned to his command tent he could smell the hot food of breakfast, and see Gladstone directing officers with their duties. Gladstone looked up as he approached.

"I don't think it will take as long as yesterday to be moving today," he said to Peabody as he came within earshot, "I think after yesterday everyone is just about ready to get back to Kleve and see if we can get this thing over, whatever that brings!"

*****

The knock on the door bought Tagan back from his thoughts, it was still early morning, and very few people would be walking the corridors of the palace. Servants at this time of day would most likely open the door to look in to see if it was clear before entering, knocking would disturb the sleep of the occupants! So it was with interest Tagan called,

"Come in." The door opened and Tagan was surprised to see Mortimer walking in,

"I hope I'm not disturbing you," he said as he entered, "but I have had this disturbing thought which I just cannot get rid of!"

"No I was awake already, I have been thinking too," Tagan replied, "how can I be of assistance?"

Mortimer sat down opposite Tagan, he then took a deep breath as if to steady his thoughts.

"I was thinking, and it looks as if your thoughts may have been on the same lines, about the Golden Griffin," Mortimer said as he pointed towards the golden medallion which Tagan was twisting between the fingers of his right hand. The medallion was said to be the sign of a Golden Griffin, and that one was Aaron's Mortimer had taken it from Aaron's body after he had been killed and had passed to on to Tagan when they were in the cave at the top of a mountain, along with the Granit Sword, a very special and supposable magical sword.

Tagan immediately stopped twisting the medallion, which he had not realised he was, but it was true, he had been thinking about a Golden Griffin.

"I was thinking," Tagan said, "if we find a person who is wearing a golden medallion, like this one, that person could be the Golden Griffin, all we would have to do is wait for them to change?"

"I can see, to some point your logic, but I don't think as a plan it will work. We know that a Golden Griffin, when they are human do not know of their other existence, and we do not know if all medallions look the same. But most of all we do not know if there are any Golden Griffin out there, Aaron may have been the last, Death hinted as much!" Mortimer said. Tagan sighed, standing up he walked around his apartment, searching for answers.

"So where do we find a Golden Griffin?" Tagan asked almost to himself. Mortimer closed his eyes, was Tagan not listening to him.

"Do you not think the question we should be asking is why the Destroyers have creatures gone across the desert to the Dark Forest?" Tagan stopped pacing and looked at Mortimer.

"I thought we had already discussed that, do you have any more questions?"

"Well, there is one that has sprung to mind," Mortimer said, "if as you say there could be another Golden Griffin, could it be that the creatures, who come from the mythical type world also know there is another Golden Griffin yet to reveal its self, and as they may not know where it is. The trap, which we all believe they have set and we are going to spring, could be to catch that Griffin, and we could be taking it right into it!"

"So you think we could already have the Golden Griffin in human form with us now, and the creatures already know that, they just do not know who it is." Tagan said slowly, Mortimer nodded,

"It's possible," he said,

"And we could be taking the Golden Griffin strait to them into their trap!" Tagan stopped, looking at Mortimer in alarm he said, "We must tell Sylvester immediately!"

Chapter 6

Faith walked the empty corridors of the Fairy world in the Dark Forest, she was not alone, a detachment of the Royal Guard, in escort saw to that, but she felt it. The ornately worked floors, walls and ceilings of the wooden trees shaped by very, very old magic was both ore inspiring and frightening to her. She had thought many times on what Tim had said to her when he was trying to rescue her from his perceived danger of the Dark Forest, that it was the centre of magic in the world. Well it probably was, but that was not a bad thing! Magic was real, she knew that, she had all her life, and Fairies were the custodians of magic. Her father the King and she, as the Royal Princess, the hair to the throne were there to protect the world from the excises and dangers of the abuse of magic that was why she, all the Fairies and the Dark Forest excited!

So that could be why the creatures were surrounding the Dark Forest, or the Destroyer's creatures as Tagan had named them, to find magic. It could also be the reason her father and his advisers seemed to be so confident that the creatures would do nothing and the Dark Forest was safe, powerful magic protecting them. She loved, and trusted her father to do the right thing, but she also knew he was very ill, so therefore venerable. Before she realised it she was outside his apartment, two guards standing rigidly at attention either side of the door. They looked at her, but did not attempted to block her way, her own escort also did not attempt to entire but took up positions the other side of the corridor.

Slowly pushing open the door without knocking she peered into the room before entering. This was the outer reception room in the large apartment, she had been born in this apartment, as had her brother Avtur, and she would move back into it when she ascended the throne. The room was large with little furniture, but long tapestries covered the walls, at the far end were two doors, Faith knew one lead to the main sitting room and the other to the sleeping apartment. It was to this door to which she made her way.

This corridor was smaller than the main ones, but still quite long with doors on both sides at regular intervals. She headed towards the third door on the right hand side of the corridor. This door looked no different than the rest, other than both the doors either side were open, this was for medical staff and attendants to be at close call for the King.

Knocking lightly she entered without waiting for an answer. The first thing that struck her was the smell, anti-septic hung in the air, every single thing had to be so clean, the fear of the King getting an infection was very real, he had been very ill and frail for quite some time, and his age was not in his favour, Faith's age hid the fact that her father had been quite old when her brother Avtur was born, and he had been at least ten years older than her when he had been killed.

Sitting on a small stool next to her father, she looked at him. He looked thin and frail, not the strong confident man who she could see in her mind's eye of her childhood, she remembered a happy upbringing, what seemed a care free childhood. She smiled to herself as she remembered. Reaching out, she took his small bony hand in hers.

"Oh Faith it's you," she heard the soft quiet voice of her father say.

"Sorry father, I did not mean to wake you," she replied,

"Wake me I should hope you did, I spend too much time sleeping now days, and it has been too long since I saw you last." He said.

"It was only yesterday since I last saw you father," she said as she gave his hand a slight squeeze,

"Only yesterday, was it?" he asked. "Well, all the days seem to run into one. Tell me my girl, what is happening outside my room in the forest?"

She did want to ask his advice and questions about what the creatures, but hesitated, after all he was very old and very ill, and the last thing she wanted to do was make his illness worse. Seeing her hesitation he said,

"You don't have to worry about me my dear, I have no intention of dying just yet."

"Well father, the Dark Forest is still surrounded, but the creatures have not entered it yet, as far as we know. But I am worried, I have given orders to form a small army but the Star Chamber will not support me in this." She said, she looked in alarm as he coughed several times, taking a cup of water she held it up for him to drink, then felt relief as she saw a smile on his face and realised he was laughing.

"An army you say? Well the Dark Forest has never had an army, where are you going to find all the Fairies to make up this army?" he asked when he had caught his breath.

"Only a small one, father of about five thousand" she replied, "we have a lot of fairies from the clans now, and I think we should be able to defend ourselves if we need to, and not rely on other people." She hoped the determined look on her face relayed how she really felt, and did not give the impression of a pouting child.

"Very well," her father said after looking at her for what seemed an age, "I will speak to the Star Chamber, a small army may be just what we need. But be under no illusion we have ever needed to rely on any one to help us, as you may soon learn!"

They spoke for a long time into the late evening, only being distracted by the occasional nurse checking on the

Kings well-being and then a stop for his dinner. The time seemed to fly passed, she could not remember the last time her father seemed to be so willing and indeed able to talk, it was just like her childhood when she did not have a care in the world. This made it even more of a wrench when the senior consultant came in and recommended the King take some sleep. Kissing her father on the forehead, Faith wished him a good night, as she looked back at him just before closing the door behind her she saw his eyes were already closed as if sleep had already taken him.

Back in the corridor, lanterns had already been lit, flames reflecting from the highly polished walls and ceiling. Her escort dropped in behind her without any words being exchanged, which was how it remained until she entered the familiar door of her own apartment.

She was slightly disappointed to see Chancellor Becket and Berberdoff sitting in two large easy chairs talking to each other in the reception room of her apartment, both immediately stopped what they had been saying on seeing her arrival and stood up.

"Please, please sit down both of you," she said to them, as a servant took her outer cloak and offered her a goblet of wine which she declined but asked for something light to eat, she had just realised just how hungry she felt. Walking over to where they had both now sat back down she took a high backed chair equal distance between them, this was a deliberate act so neither could think she was favouring them. After a short silence to allow her to settle and compose herself, Becket coughed to clear his throat and then said.

"If I may ask Princess, how is your father today?" Faith smiled to herself, this was Chancellor Becket at his political best, easing her into a conversation with simple questions which she would feel happy with and willing to give open answers without having to think, then as she let her guard slip, the difficult questions, which may trip her up! But Faith was also a politician, no, she was not openly political, she was not allowed to be, but she had grown up as a member of her Royal family, and politics was deep in her blood.

"He is as well as can be expected thank you Chancellor, given his age," she replied and before another question was shot in her direction she added, "And he has approved the idea of a small army for the Dark Forest, he said he will talk to the Star Chamber and express his feeling the next time they meet."

"That is good news Royal Princess," Berberdoff said, from the other chair, "I take it you will now tell Prince Avtag to start the recruitment and training?"

"I believe he has started that already, but he calls it expansion, not recruitment, he said it sounds less confrontational!" Faith said.

"Well we also have some positive news, Royal Princess," Becket said slightly leaning forward as if not to speak too load, "we have found three girls who are willing and we believe able to fly to Kleve and deliver a message, and at least two of them will be able to fly back with a reply." Faith who was glad to hear the news suddenly felt a stab of worry by the last part.

"What do you mean by only two returning, what will happen to the third one?" she asked.

"Well Royal Princess," Berberdoff said, "two of the fairies come from my clan, they have discovered that they can fly higher, a lot higher than fairies from the Dark Forest, the other one is from the Dark Forest. We think that the three of them would be able to slip passed the flying creatures by a slight diversion which they are planning. But they would not be able plan a similar diversion for the return trip." Faith nodded taking everything he said in. "Clan Fairies can not only fly higher than Dark Forest Fairies, which we think is at about the same height as the flying creatures, but higher of course than the creatures, so when they return they can just fly over the creatures untll they are over the Dark Forest and then descend in safety. The Fairy, who goes from the Dark Forest to deliver the message, simply stays in Kleve or with the army until she thinks it safe to make the return."

"Why, if there is problems with how high Fairies from the Dark Forest fly. not just send the two from the clan?" Faith asked.

"Because Berberdoff thinks the people in Kleve may think the two Fairies sent from the clan may be a trap." Becket said. Faith looked at Berberdoff with a questioning face, and he nodded in agreement. Then said,

"When we were in Kleve you may remembered Royal Princess some words of mistrust were said, by myself I will admit, and by others of the clan Fairies about the Dark Forest and its Fairies, and at that time we had lost the ability to fly. For two clan Fairies to suddenly turn up saying the Dark Forest needs help and being able to fly may be just too much. They would probably believe it was a trap!"

Faith did remember, and at the time also remembered being quite hurt by the comments which had been passed onto her by Mortimer, so the plan of sending three seemed to be a good one, so why did she feel a bit of hesitation from the two men?

"When are they leaving?" she asked.

"Well we are still working on the diversion plan, we don't want it to fail before it starts, and we need to give the girls a good start, but also flying is very new to clan Fairies, so they have to just get used to it and practices as much as they can." Becket replied.

"What is this plan and how are these girls preparing?" Faith asked.

It was at this point both men lent forward to speak in very low voices, so no one outside the room or even at the sides of the room would be able to hear, Faith lent forward too.

The plan was to encourage as many of the clan Fairies to try flying as possible, this was not very difficult to accomplish as they all seemed to want to fly. They would keep within the area of the Dark Forest so as to not disturb the surrounding creatures, however some of the Fairies would at great height "wonder" a little further afield, in this way they could see what was happening outside the surrounding creatures and get the creatures used to the Fairies flying over them without threatening them. The plan sounded good and Faith could immediately see benefits for her new army in using the clan Fairies height, but kept them to herself, for the time being.

"Who else knows what you are planning?" Faith asked.

"Us three and the three girls," Berberdoff replied.

"Good, let us keep it that way," Faith said, "the less people who know, the less chance of it all unravelling." Then leaping to her feet, she walked to a table set with cold foods, taking some meat and fruit as she realised just how hungry she felt.

Sensing the meeting was over Chancellor Becket and Berberdoff also got to their feet.

"Please keep me informed of any developments," she said, but then added, "I will not meet these girls, I do not want any undue attention towards them, I will of course meet them all when this is over to thank them, but until then I do not want anyone suspecting I know anything of this, never mind approving it, is that clear?"

"Quite clear and an utterly sensible course of action," Becket said.

The two men then gave Faith a nodded bow and together left the room, Faith could hear the outer apartment door close as they bid goodnight to a servant who was holding the door for them.

Faith taking some more food on a plate went and sat beck down on the seat which she had been occupying, the meeting and plans running around her head. Her father and seeing him, she did not know if she liked all this sub diffusion, she would have liked a simpler life, hopefully, she smiled to herself with Tagan, but since the death of Avtur she had responsibilities. Then a thought struck her, where was Death? She had not seen him in an age, and he seemed to pop up at the most inappropriate times, but now nothing, and if she needed his advice, now was probably the most appropriate time. With this thought now joining all the others running around her head she settled down, sleep was not something she thought she would see much of tonight.

Chapter 7

"Where are we going in such a hurry so early in the morning?" Mortimer asked between gasps of breath, although he was old he did have a habit of early rising, and now days that involved going and speaking to Prince Tagan who did not seem to sleep. But Tagan did sleep, very well in fact, and it was when he slept that his mind wondered and he seemed to have some of his best thoughts, and this was one such time. He was waiting for the knock on the door from Mortimer which he was sure would come, and when it did he was ready to go.

"We are going to see the Council of Ten," Tagan said glancing back at the older man without breaking his stride.

"Wait, wait," Mortimer said suddenly stopping, "why are we hurrying to go and see the Council of Ten? If I remember the last time they were not too forthcoming until Death opened their eyes!"

"Yes," Tagan said, also stopping and turning back to face Mortimer, "but they did put us on the right track, they must have seen something which set us on the right course. "Now we all think we know all the answers, but do we really, do we know why the creatures have gone into the desert and surrounded the Dark Forest, do we know if there is another Golden Griffin and where to find it?"

"And you believe they will have the answers?" Mortimer asked, Tagan shrugged his shoulders,

"I don't know, and neither will you until we ask them!" He then turned and started walking at the same pace as before, with a slight shake of his head Mortimer joined him.

The building in which the Council sat was imposing, set at the far end of a very open square the front of the building was dominated by a set of large doors, far too big for the size of the building and far too big to be practical, a group of mounted horsemen could enter six abreast and still have plenty of room! This was built to impress, to intimidate whoever approached the Council of Ten, to set out the order of authority before the petitioner had even entered the building, and it worked!

Banging on the front doors as hard as he could with the hilt of his sword Tagan stood back to wait for a reaction. A few moments later, the seemingly smallest movement slightly cracked open the doors. Giving Mortimer an encouraging smile Tagan approached the small opening of the doors. The impression was he would have to squeeze though, but he found he had plenty of room, Mortimer followed, then as if by magic the great doors closed again.

Tagan looked around, the chamber room in which the y stood was as large in proportions as the doors were on the outside, windows from the tops of the walls flooded the room with early morning light, very different from when they had first visited the Council for advice!

Sitting high up in grand chairs were the members of the Council, the Ten most brilliant and knowledgeable minds in Mercia, not part of the constitution of Mercia, but it would be a very stupid monarch to ignore their advice! Mortimer had once been mentioned as being a potential member but for some reason which Tagan had never found out, and Mortimer never talked about, he had never been asked. If he resented this or was happy was hard to tell due to his self-important and arrogant behaviour.

Silence filled the room, only being broken by the shuffling of Tagan and Mortimer's boots on the polished stone floor.

"And what do we have the honour of this visit your Highness?" An old but steady voice asked from above their heads. Tagan and Mortimer turned to where the voice had come from to answer, but both knew the next member of the Council to speak would more than likely be from behind them.

"We are seeking advice on how we should proceed against the Destroyer's Creatures, they have surrounded the Dark Forest, and Aaron the Golden Griffin is dead: my question is. Is this a trap, and do we need to find another Golden Griffin to be able to defeat the Destroyer and his creatures?" Tagan said, with Mortimer adding in a mutter beside him,

"Is there another Golden Griffin to even find?"

A slight noise could be heard from above them, almost a humming, but then it abruptly stopped!

"Where is Death?" A sharp voice asked from the other side of the room.

"That was another question we hoped you could help us with," Tagan said, turning to the unknown voice, "we have not seen him for quite some time, and although it sounds slightly strange, I for one am worried."

"This is very serious!" The same voice said.

"How can the living live if Death is absent?" Another voice asked almost at the same time, Mortimer had a worried expression on his face as he leaned close to Tagan's ear to whisper,

"I'm very concerned, the Council always keeps a very disciplined hold on their emotions, and never ever express concerns." Tagan looking up to the unseen faces said.

"Life is going on, people are still dying, if that makes you happy, and I suppose, although I have not seen it myself, babies are still being born. Death is always here, we just have not seen him in person for a time."

"You show your ignorance Prince Tagan, and I am disappointed in you Mortimer I would have thought you would have grasped the situation a lot sooner," a booming voice full of authority said, "the absence of Death is not just unfortunate, it strikes at the very centre of life. The Destroyer is attacking the world in many ways now. In answer to your questions we can give none, I wish we could, but dreams have not been forthcoming so we have none to interpret. My advice to you is, go where you first set foot on this quest together go there and you may get answers." Shouts filled the chamber from the unseen Councillors, suddenly silenced by a hard knock!

"THIS IS TOO IMPORTANT TO PLAY POLITICS WITH" the same voice said in a load deliberate tone, then adding, a little softer, "Your destiny and that of your friends are now more than ever entwined with that of the world. Time is running out so make all your decisions count, you have too little time to make errors!"

The two large main doors suddenly began to swing open, Tagan looked up to catch a glimpse of any of the Councillors, and he still had questions which needed answers.

"I think that is our cue to leave," Mortimer said from beside him. Reluctantly he followed Mortimer outside as they stepped back into the square the doors closed behind them, not a sound.

"Well what now?" Tagan said.

"I think they suggested we go and ask the Seeker of Truth again," Mortimer replied.

"You may well be right," Tagan said, "but that will take us months and in the wrong direction, do we have that much time?"

"That, I do not know, but what I do know is that it was the Seeker who revealed Aaron as the Golden Griffin, I think if anyone can help us he can."

*****

The Champion Lord walked the corridors of the Royal Palace with confidence, it was another world when he had been attacked by a creature and saved by Captain Bulwick, which had cost him his life. Now Tim had an escort of the Wildbloods, the best trained, bravest and experienced Guardians there were, as well as Stickleback Guardian his General commanding the Guardian and Major Lord Bazzington who commanded his human cavalry. Megan, for nearly the first time since he had met her was not with him, which he had not realised he would miss so much, but she had said she had an audience with the Queen. He however had been summoned by Field Marshal Roderick Sylvester Hungerford, the commander of the Allied Army and for the want of a better word, his boss for the forthcoming campaign.

The main briefing room, which the Field Marshal used for all his planning was a noisy hive of activity, Tim could not help but notice as the main door was opened for him. He saw soldiers with bundles of papers hurrying between desks occupied by other soldiers scribing away, a very large map on the wall showed every detail of the forth coming campaign. The whole professionalism and industry of the planning was very impressive, if it was a foretaste of the future, Tim felt a little more relaxed.

"Ah, my Champion Lord," Sylvester said, looking up from a handful of reports as he heard the door open, "thank you for attending so quickly."

"You summonsed me, did I have any choice?" Tim replied with an off-handed tone. The Field Marshal gave Tim a withering stare, but did not rise to the challenge.

"I know you have heard reports like this one, but we now have a detailed description of one of the caves in which the creatures multiply. I would appreciate it if you and your commanders would take a detailed look at it." Sylvester said, offering a folded, but well used piece of paper to Tim. Tim took the paper and opened it very carefully.

"You can use one of the desks over there," Sylvester said pointing to a few unoccupied desks near to the foot of the large map. Tim nodded an acknowledgement, and as he began to read the report, made his way towards the desk, where he laid the report down to enable Stickleback and Bazzington to also read it.

As Tim read he could feel his stomach churning at the details, but he kept reading, making sure he had committed to memory every single detail of the report. When he was satisfied he had taken it all in he sat back on a stool, the feeling of sickness at the pit of his stomach was the overriding sensation which enveloped him as he thought about what he had just read. A few moments latter both Stickleback and Bazzington also sat back, not a word was said, Stickleback's insect face was impossible for Tim to read, but Bazzington's was pale and almost sickly, Tim could read clearly the effect which the report had had on him!

"I think that shows clearly exactly just what an evil enemy we are fighting and just this enemy is capable of," Sylvester said quietly from beside Tim, he had got up from his desk and joined them, unnoticed as they had been engrossed in the devastating reports.

"I notice from the report that the cave is being guarded from the outside, but there seem to be grounds to think some of the cocoons could still open." Stickleback was the first to speak.

"Yes that is right and it is the reason I have asked you to come here today." Sylvester replied, "You see, and I'll come straight to the point, the occupants of those cocoons must be killed! Whatever they used to be, they are now developing into creatures, and we do not know how this comes about or when they stop being human. But we do know what they are when they emerge! So the only real option is to kill them before they do so, and that is why I have asked you here."

"So you think the Guardian is suitable for this inhuman task?" Tim asked with a bitter tone to his voice.

"I know the task is inhuman, but it is one we must do," Sylvester replied in a low voice, "I was wondering if the Guardian had the same feelings as humans?"

"No we do not," Stickleback said before Tim could reply, "and yes it is an unpleasant task, even for us, but we are quite capable of completing it quickly and without fuss, with your permission, Champion Lord, I will dispatch some flying wings to complete the task?"

Before Tim could reply the door opened revealing two very scruffy looking officers and an older looking woman. All appeared very hot, sweaty and dusty as if they had been riding hard for several days.

The more senior in rank of the two officers, a colonel Tim thought, spoke: "Field Marshal, Sir, we got here as fast as we could travel, General Flintlock and the army of Greater Longmans who we met on our journey, will be joining us soon."

"Very good Colonel, you have made good time," Sylvester said, and then turning to Tim he said, "Champion Lord, may I introduce Colonel Peabody, he is the author of the report which you have just read, and along with Major Gladstone the commander of a very unique regiment. My plan is for you to command Major Gladstone and his regiment with the Guardian and your Lancers."

Tim offered his hand to Peabody, who shook it,

"A very thorough report Colonel although not pleasant to read," Tim said, then added, "Why did the Field Marshal describe your regiment as unique?"

"Well Sir, about three quarters of my soldiers are women." Peabody replied.

"Interesting," Tim said, "We will talk later, when we have dealt with the problem with what you found in the cave." Then turning to Stickleback said, "If you think some of the flying Guardian are suitable for this task I will bow to your judgment, you might as well dispatch them as soon as possible, there is no reason to delay such a gruesome task."

"Yes, my Champion Lord," Stickleback said, then turned and quickly walked out of the briefing room with a few of the escort.

"Colonel," Sylvester said, after Stickleback left, "this young lady you have with you, you have not introduced her yet."

"I'm sorry Sir" Peabody replied as Willow, a slight smile at being called a young lady stepped forward, "May I introduce Willow, she was the head of the women's council in her village."

"Welcome Willow," Sylvester said, "I am Sylvester, I take it from your presence that all the women from your village have travelled to Kleve, not just the ones who wish to fight?"

"That is correct Sir," Willow said, "We could not leave anyone behind, and we all wish to serve."

"Thank you, I'm glad to hear that, and I assure you that all your women will be found useful jobs in our army, there is much a non-fighting woman can contribute to improve the lot for all," Sylvester said, "I will speak to you soon in more detail, but in the meantime if you could ask your ladies were they think their skills could be of most service."

Willow replied she would, and on Peabody's signal the two officers and Willow left. The briefing room was left in an industrious hum of Clarks scribing over their notes and reading reports, all keeping a respectful silence for the most part. Tim took the time to study the large map on the wall of the desert and the Dark Forest, most details were missing, but they seemed to be slowly getting filled in.

The door opening broke Tim's concentration, he looked up to see Tagan and Mortimer enter, both looked flustered, as if they had been hurrying. Tagan looked around the room as if searching for someone, he nodded as his eyes fell on Tim, but made no movement forward. But as he saw Sylvester he quickly said something to Mortimer and both men made their way towards him.

Sylvester was sitting just behind where Tim stood, so as Tagan's behaviour intrigued him he turned around so he could hear what was about to be said.

"Sylvester," Tagan said, "we have been looking for you," as he drew close. Sylvester stopped what he was reading and slowly looked at Tagan and Mortimer, he seemed to be weighing up what he wanted to say to them, but he put the report which he had been reading down and said,

"Well, Your Highness, you couldn't have been looking that hard, as I've been here every day for almost a month making plans." His eyes glowed with anger as he spoke.

"Yes, of course, I'm sorry," Tagan replied, "but we have been thinking and as a result this morning we have visited the Council of Ten."

"The Council of Ten," Sylvester said, "who might they be?"

"They are the most learned thinkers in Mercia," Mortimer answered.

Sylvester nodded his thanks, then asked, "And what wisdom did they express?"

"They told us we should go to the Seeker of Truth to ask him questions and he may be able to give us the answers." Tagan said. Tim did not know what reaction Tagan and Mortimer were expecting, but he did not think it was the one they got. Sylvester just looked at them both for a time, then with the slightest shake of his head he picked up the report he had been reading again.

"Did you hear what I just said?" Tagan asked,

"Yes I did," Sylvester replied, then added, "It's a long way, when do you intend to leave?"

"Do you not think it is important to go and ask him questions?" Tagan said, the atmosphere was getting tense.

"What questions?" Sylvester said, putting down his report.

"Well, is there another Golden Griffin, and are we taking it into a trap, what has happened to Death, why have the creatures travelled all the way across the desert to the Dark Forest?"

"Is there another Golden Griffin to be discovered? I don't know, so I'm planning on the grounds there is not. Are we going into a trap? Yes. What has happened to Death and why have the creatures surrounded the Dark Forest? Again I do not know, but I can tell you this, the Dark Forest is the place to get the answers - all the answers!" He turned to face Tagan and Mortimer with a look of rage which was barely contained.

"I am really disappointed in you both, especially you Mortimer. I thought you had more common sense, more intelligence. The Seeker is a mystic, he may at times give good answers, or answers which in time turn out right. But I work on facts and what I can see. There are too many lives are at stake for me to even think about airy fairy words and theories. If you want to go and ask him your questions I cannot and will not stop you, but we will not be here when you return."

"But the Seeker did reveal Aaron," Mortimer said. A cutting look from Sylvester stopped Mortimer from speaking further. Tagan held up his hand slightly.

"I quite understand Sylvester, and we will endeavour to help you in any way we can." Tagan said, then seeing Mortimer wanting to say more added, "we will leave you to get on with your work, I'm sorry." Then he turned and with Mortimer following walked out of the room in silence.

Tim desperately wanted to speak, but looking at Sylvester, who had returned to reading reports again, he thought better of it. But he did have a feeling of security for the oncoming campaign.

Chapter 8

Tim almost felt like skipping back to his apartment in the palace, he was laughing to himself about the encounter he had just witnessed between the Field Marshal and Prince Tagan. He respected Tagan, was even in ore of him, so seeing him being put in his place so precisely was quite an experience for Tim, and now he wanted to share that with Megan.

As he opened the apartment door leaving his escort outside, any thoughts of telling Megan what had just occurred evaporated, sitting on a couch opposite Megan, and holding a conversation with her was the Queen, a quick scan of the room showed him they were not alone but Baroness Heartfelt was also in the room, standing by the buffet helping herself to a glass of wine.

As they realised Tim had entered the room, the conversation stopped. Looking at him with a smile, Megan said, "Aah, Tim, you're back. We have company - may I introduce Her Majesty, Queen Kathryn and Baroness Heartfelt."

Tim bowed to the Queen, "Your Majesty, it is my honour," then turning to the Baroness, "It is good to see you again Baroness, you look as elegant as ever."

"He really is a charmer now days," the Baroness said as she took her wine along with another glass which she walked over and gave the Queen, before sitting down on an empty chair, "I think you will have to keep a close eye on him Princess,"

"I fully intend to." Megan replied, the smile never slipping from her face. Tim had the idea he had just stepped into the den of three she wolves and he was the prey.

"But just remember, Megan," the Queen said, "Sir Timothy is a slippery character, he should be my messenger but he now seems to have given himself other titles."

"I'm...." Tim was just starting to speak when Megan cut him off with a cutting look.

"I do not believe Tim has given himself titles, Your Majesty, I rather think it is his destiny, which you with your kind patronage have helped fore fill." An uneasy silence momentarily filled the room. Tim felt it could be cut but also felt if he was to speak the atmosphere would be very, very unpleasant for him. He seemed to be the intruder in a conversation about him, to which he was unwelcome, as if two lionesses were making out their territory under the guidance of an older wiser great aunt.

"Your Majesty," Baroness Heartfelt said slowly, "I do not believe Sir Timothy has betrayed you in any way. In fact you could say he has enhanced your authority, after all he has bought an army to help relieve Kleve, and is still showing you dutiful respect. He is also now under the leadership of your brother Prince Tagan, none of which would give me the impression he is, or wants to betray you. I do agree with Princess Megan, a lot has happened since we let Tim out into the world, he has served Prince Tagan loyally and at some point he has for a reason which I do not understand taken up a position of leadership of his own, and been named the Champion Lord by those who follow him. My advice Your Majesty if you would be willing to accept, would be either ignore the situation, or embrace it."

The Queen, who seemed to be listening to every word intently, nodded slowly. She looked at Tim, weighing him up in her mind, Tim felt as if he was prey being assessed for food. Suddenly the Queen bounded to her feet in a very unroyal fashion, taking everyone by surprise.

"Very well, Baroness Heartfelt I also can see no betrayal or plotting," The Queen said, and then turning to Tim, "Sir Timothy tomorrow at noon you will attend me in the Great Throne room, accompanied by all your sponsors and entourage. There I will ennoble you correctly in the eyes of Mercia, if you will accept?"

Tim felt a little shocked at the Queens announcement, Megan, who was now standing, radiated a beaming smile which was duplicated by the Baroness. Tim gave the Queen a deep and deliberate bow, with the entire flourish which he had been taught,

"I would be honoured, Your Majesty." With a slight, approving glance towards Tim, the Queen swept out of the room, leaving the three in somewhat of a shocked silence.

The Baroness was the first to break the spell. "Congratulations Tim," she said, "to the best of my knowledge you will be the first to be ennobled by royal patronage in Mercia this reign." Then she took a seat opposite to where Tim and Megan had sat down, and studied them both intently with her eyes. "I must say you two do make a fine couple, but I must say I am surprised that the Queen takes such liberal attitude to an unmarried couple staying in the palace. I take it I am correct and you are not yet married?

Megan nearly choked on hearing what the Baroness had just said, and with a reddening face spurted out, "No, we are not married, and yes, we do share this apartment. But Baroness Heartfelt I do not know what you take us for, I sleep in my room there, and the Champion Lord sleeps in his bedroom over there." Pointing to an open door on the other side of the apartment, the Baroness looked embarrassed.

"I am so sorry," she said before standing, then looking at Tim, "Sir Timothy, or should I say, Champion Lord, I am very proud of you, you have come a long way since we first met with Captain Trumpeter, and I must add I was very saddened to hear of his death." Then turning back towards Megan, she said, "Princess, again I apologise for any misunderstandings, I am glad we met and I am sure you will be nothing but good for Tim." Then with a quick nod to them both she quickly walked out of the apartment door.

"Well I never," Megan said, but before she could say anything else Tim burst out with.

"Tagan and Mortimer were just put right into their boxes by the Field Marshal!" Megan, still keeping a look of supreme calmness said,

"What on Earth are you talking about?"

Between bouts of laughter, Tim explained to Megan the conversation which he had heard in the briefing room between Tagan, Mortimer and Field Marshal Hungerford. When he had finished retelling the tale, Megan too was holding her sides with laughter.

*****

Tagan was surprised to see his sister, the Queen wondering the palace corridors alone and even more so to see the smile that spread across her face from cheek to cheek.

"You look very pleased with yourself, Katheryn," he said as he and Mortimer caught up with her.

Looking at them both, one at a time as if summing up their mood, she replied, "I am, I have just solved the problem of the Champion Lord." Tagan gave her a worried look while Mortimer's face held an expression of interest.

"I did not know there was a problem with the Champion Lord?" Tagan asked.

"Well you may not have seen the problem, but as Queen I could see a problem of people just giving themselves titles, Tim himself seems a very nice boy, but I made him a Knight, on your request if I remember correctly, and now he has just made himself a Lord." The Queen said.

Both Tagan and Mortimer stopped walking, and when the Queen realised they were not with her she also stopped and looked back at them,

"What have you done?" Tagan said.

"I have told Tim I well ennoble him," the Queen replied.

"But you can't do that." Mortimer burst out, and then seemed to regret his outburst as soon as he had said it. Tagan gave him a withering look, but it was nothing in comparison to the expression on the Queen's face.

"I think Mortimer," the Queen said in a cold flat voice while stepping up very close to him, "You forget yourself. If, and only if, I want your advice I will ask for it but until I do, you will remember your position."

"I think what Mortimer was implying is that this is a very big decision which could have unforeseen circumstances," Tagan quickly said.

The Queen, without stepping away from Mortimer, looked at Tagan. "What unforeseen circumstances?" she asked, Tagan looked around the corridor, it was almost empty, but a palace was a hot bed of gossip.

"I think we should go somewhere a little less open," he said. Soon they were all standing in Mortimer's apartment, it was the smallest, but also the closest. The Queen, immediately on entering, sat down without being asked, as if reinforcing her authority, Tagan, after looking at Mortimer who just shrugged his shoulders did the same, then Mortimer sat last, but still looking unsure.

"So what are these unforeseen circumstances?" The Queen asked, with a voice full of contempt.

"Well if you don't mind, I think Mortimer would be the best qualified to explain." Tagan said. The Queen gave Tagan a sweet smile and slight nod to accept the advice, but hard, cold eyes fell on Mortimer. Mortimer inwardly smiled. He was now getting used to the company he found himself in and the Queen's attempt to intimidate him was beginning to lose its effect.

"Your Majesty, the problem is this, the Champion Lord is not yours to give, it comes from the Guardian, they decide who the Champion Lord is, and they have decided on Tim."

Tagan sat back waiting for the back lash, but it did not come, instead the Queen looked on with a concerned expression.

"The problem I have Mortimer," the Queen began to say, "is everyone knows I made Tim a Knight, now he has returned, yes with the Guardian, but calling himself the Champion Lord - it appears to undermine my authority."

Tagan could see his sister's problem and from the expression on Mortimer's face, Mortimer seemed to be struggling with the problem in his head.

"I quite understand Your Majesty," Mortimer replied after what seemed like a long time, "when, may I ask do you intend to ennoble Tim?"

"Tomorrow at noon, I have told him to be accompanied by all his sponsors, who I of course mean the Guardian." The Queen replied, and then waited for an answer, which did not seem immediately forthcoming.

Then Mortimer eventually looked up. "Very good Your Majesty, if I may I will have to think on this, but I believe this may be able to work very well, do I have your permission to have a free hand on this and your authority to call on any resources available?" Mortimer asked.

"Yes you have," the Queen replied, "but I must approve any plan before you set it into motion," the Queen said.

"Yes, of course," Mortimer replied.

The Queen rose and without speaking left the apartment leaving Mortimer deep in thought planning for the next day with Tagan feeling a little left out.

Chapter 9

It was quite late at night, the lit lanterns casting shadows across the corridor, when Tagan found himself outside the briefing room, he had not meant to gravitate here following the mornings incident, but Mortimer had seemed consumed by all of his planning, so Tagan, who could see he was not going to be called on for his opinion, thought it best to use his spare time to clear the air with Sylvester again.

Taking a deep breath, Tagan - feeling apprehensive, slowly pushed open the door. Tagan was not used to apologising not because he did not ever feel he had to but because he tried to never put himself in such a position as to merit an apology, however, Tagan knew an apology was now required. The briefing room was quite dark and only lit by lanterns on the occupied desks (of which there were few), none of the wall mounted lanterns were lit. The desk lanterns cast shadows against the walls from the few bodies that were in the room, the shadows were large and disturbing and unnerved Tagan in a way he could not explain.

The general sense of gloom filling the room was broken only by four excited voices standing around the most central desk with a candle casting their shadows. Tagan knew two of the voices without seeing their faces, Sylvester and Cogan, the light from the candle also illuminated their faces showing clearly their entire feature's to Tagan, but the other two men were a mystery to him.

As the main briefing room door clicked shut behind him, the conversation stopped and all four men stopped talking and looked towards him, as if trying to split the darkness with their searching eyes to identify the intruder. Tagan feeling no fear in his own briefing room walked forward confidently, at a steady pace.

"Arh Prince Tagan, your timing could not have been judged better," Sylvester said as soon as the light was sufficient for Tagan to be properly seen, "May I introduce General Flintlock and Major Arawn, his Aid decamp, they are of the Greater Longmans Army."

"I am very glad to meet you," Tagan said extending his hand in welcome, "I am Tagan of Mercia. It is not the first time we have had an army from Greater Longmans, did you know Grand Duke Danneh and Grand Duke Ynyr?"

"No Prince Tagan I do not know them personally but I do know of them and that is the reason I am here," General Flintlock said.

Lord Cogan explained that the General was leading a combined army of both Greater Longmans and Mercia to investigate the reason for the massacre and to confront the Destroyer's creatures. However, instead of finding answers they had found a regiment, which Field Marshal Hungerford had sent, who were on a mission to try to discover the same answers. All the armies had joined up to return to Kleve and on their journey had discovered some caves.

"I will show you the reports on the caves, which I am sure you will find quite disturbing - I know I did." Sylvester said to Tagan when Cogan had finished speaking.

"Thank you," Tagan replied, then asked, "I remember you saying the troops we had were all we needed to take on this campaign, as every extra soldier would need, something like six or eight extra support staff, what has changed?"

"I think, if I may reply," General Flintlock said, "quite a lot has changed," Sylvester nodded his approval and the General continued.

"First, we have quite a stake in this, we have already contributed an army which combined with one of yours was sent to fight the creatures, and as you know destroyed."

Tagan nodded his understanding.

"Secondly, what we discovered in the caves, which I have heard the Field Marshal tell you he will show you the reports, so if you do not mind I will not go over again and thirdly and most practically, you need us!" Tagan was quite shocked by this last statement, because he had heard Sylvester's plans and they seemed quite adequate, before Tagan could ask the question which was on his lips.

Sylvester said, "It's our tail, we are quite venerable in our logistics tail, and the General quite correctly pointed this out. So he has volunteered to use his army not to fight in the battle, but to perform the very unglamorous task of guarding our tail as we move across the desert and fight the battle."

Tagan was quite surprised, both by the General's generosity and the seemingly oversight by Sylvester.

"Well General I thank you and welcome you," Tagan said. The General then talked for a little longer to the three of them, then deciding it was late, and he would have a lot of plans to put into place before the campaign started, he bid them a good night, he and Major Arawn left.

Tagan tried to take this opportunity to speak to Sylvester with only Lord Cogan there, but as soon as he began to speak Sylvester waved him away.

"What has been has been," he said, "we have too much to be planning, in what is now a short time to be going over old ground, if you have the time tomorrow I would like you to look at some problems we have to overcome, and I believe we all have an audience with the Queen at midday."

Tagan was quite surprised Sylvester already knew of the ceremony the next day, Mortimer was walking quickly, but grateful he could stop thinking about his previous error. He was in a much better mood as he made his way through the lantern lit corridors back to his apartment. It was after midnight when he finally settled into his bed, not knowing if Sylvester, Cogan or Mortimer were so lucky.

*****

It was early on a cool bright morning when Tagan found himself on the Kleve showground. The early autumnal mist was just retreating in favour of the bright sunshine, the bite of cold from the change in season was beginning to be felt.

The showground was on the south west of the city, it was made up if Earth pens and large cleared pastures. This area had been at the heart of the fighting which was now being popularly known as the Battle of Kleve, the nearby dwellings at the north edge of the showground had fared much worse: with total destruction of most of them, even this early in the morning Tagan could see the darkened figures of labours hard at work rebuilding the houses and shops, in the race against the onward marching winter.

Surrounding the showground on the south and west sides, the various armies camped, the Allied Army to the west, in rows upon rows of uniformed tents, interrupted only by larger ones for cooking and command and the picket lines of horses tethered by their regimental colours. The Greater Longmans Army by contrast laid their camp out in a circular paten, with all their houses on the outside of the camp, Tagan had been told this was only used at a "home base" and not campaign, when the horses were kept at the centre of the camp for protection from attack.

But Tagan, and the small number of staff which he had bought along with him were not here to see either army, no they were here to meet merchants, traders in camels! Sylvester had thought of an idea which he hoped would lessen the amount of water the army would use every day, or at least most days, most of the cavalry horses for all the Lancers, Hussars and the Mounted Marines would be replaced by camels, and some of the donkeys and asses. So Tagan was here to look and buy thousands of camels!

"May I ask Your Highness, if I may be so bold, if you know anything about camels?" a short tubby Captain of the newly-formed Veterinary Croup asked Tagan.

Tagan who was still enjoying the stillness of the early morning and letting his mind drift, was startled by the Captain's approach (the Captain could not have helped but notice but gave no acknowledgement of seeing).

"No I know nothing whatsoever about camels," Tagan replied with a slight grin on his face, then added, "that is why I have bought you and your staff along." The Captain nodded in reply but said nothing, Tagan knew the Captain also had no knowledge about camels, but hoped the Captain and his staff, which knew everything there was to know about horses could convince the sellers they would know if they were being sold a dud!

"They are approaching from the south east," a call came up from the assembled staff. Tagan looked in the indicated direction, squinting into the rising sun, to see great clouds of dust in the air, then the ungainly appearance of thousands of camels being herded quite fast in their direction. Very soon the whole showground seemed to be taken over by camels and flies. The Veterinary Croup staff mingling with the camel's owners, assessing the animals and splitting them into groups, then bartering for the best price. The Captain had however left the main centre of activity and attached himself to a group of the camel riders, who had now completed their task of driving the camels for sale and were receiving their wages, the negotiations here seemed as intense as any of the bartering.

Very soon most of the camels were being split into two groups - the largest in one group and the not so large in another, In order to be herded away by the Captain's staff and the camel riders. In the other direction, heading back the way they had come were some very happy and much richer, former camel owners.

"We have four thousand camels for the cavalry and another two thousand pack animals, and I'm glad to say we have secured the services of fifty of the camel riders to help us train and look after the Camels." The Captain said with a smile on his face.

"Captain you and your staff have done an excellent mornings work, what are you going to do now?" Tagan said.

"Well Sir, we will go and give our camels the quick once over, then by this afternoon I hope to be introducing them to the first of the cavalry regiments."

"Captain, again I congratulate you on a magnificent job well done, and I will delay you no longer." Tagan, returning the Captain's salute watched him depart before turning to his own mount, after settling himself onto the saddle he rode towards the Allied Camp and to the Lancers Regiment, he wondered how they would take the news that they were to replace their horses with camels, his second task for the day.

Chapter 10

The slight rushing wind gave a pleasant chill to the exposed skin on Starlight's face, arms and legs. It took away the burning sensation of the bright sun, which could be quite harsh on the skin with no cloud coverage and thin air. It was one of the first and most painful discoveries which the clan Fairies had made after they rediscovered the ability to fly at altitude. The obvious answer was to cover face, arms and legs, which Starlight did on most of the flights she undertook, but occasionally she enjoyed the feeling of the rushing wind against her skin.

Starlight's friend, Windfall was as always covered up. She wore a type of helmet which covered her entire head down to her neck and shoulders, with eye slits that made her look quite sinister. Her flying jacket and leggings were thick and padded, enabling her to maintain altitude without feeling the effects of wind-chill or heat on her skin. This light weight style of clothing seemed to have been adapted by the flyers in all the clans, giving the impression of it being a uniform. This was reinforced when it appeared in very pale pink and blue colours which seemed to have the effect of hiding the flyer, at high altitude, from anyone on the ground looking up or flying at a low height. Windfall favoured the pink version, but for today at least Starlight wore the more traditional clan dress, but with shorts instead of trousers, as if to state her independence!

"There's Dew," Windfall said pointing down, Starlight followed her directions and saw a fast moving object cutting across the desert floor, it could only be a flying Fairy at the speed and the lack of immediate dust being thrown up, but Starlight did notice a growing dust trail beginning to form a short distance behind her, a sure giveaway to anything who learnt what to look for to indicate the presence of a low fast flying Fairy.

"She is very impressive," said Starlight, admiration filling her voice as she watched the daring Fairy eating up the miles in little time, but then with concern filling her voice added, "but we will have to tell her about the dust trail which she is blowing up, it could be a matter life and death for her!"

Suddenly, the shooting figure vanished. Both Fairies looked down in shock trying to locate Dew, without a word between them they both began to descend quite rapidly scouring the desert floor far below. Starlight felt her heart pounding and a sick feeling in the pit of her stomach as she thought of the reasons of her friend's sudden disappearance.

They had descended a few thousand feet when Windfall called, "There she is, I've just seen her take off and she's flying back a lot slower, I only saw her because of her shadow!"

Starlight again looked down in the direction indicated, first she saw nothing, and was beginning to question in her mind Windfall's eyesight, but then she saw movement, slow, very slow in comparison to her last sighting, but too fast to be moving on the ground, then she noticed the shadow and it became obvious that they were indeed looking at a flying Fairy. Dew was also wearing the new type of flying clothing, this was very much like the style of clothing which had always been worn by Fairies from the Dark Forest, but made of several different shades of sand and stone. This provided camouflage when looking down from a height. Now both Windfall and Starlight had to highlight the problems to her about dust trails and shadows. These would need to be overcome or at the very list minimised.

They did not lose all their altitude until they were over the boundaries of the Dark Forest and Dew was safe and able to join them. Then together the three Fairies descended to the safety of the forest floor. They spent a short time sitting on an old tree stump discussing the day's flight and any problems which any of them had encountered, Starlight and Windfall bought up the problem of dust and shadow, Dew scemed to take it in but did not seem over alarmed about either problem.

"I suppose it's time to go and face the music with the Chancellor and Berberdoff," Windfall said. Together, the three fairies walked towards the entrance of the Dark Wood and into the corridors which connected to the Dark Forest. In no time the fairies stood outside a doorway which the three had visited many times before.

"Come in girls," the formal voice of Berberdoff called from the other side of the closed door. The three Fairies looked at each other their thoughts were all as one. It was uncanny, even spooky how he always knew they were outside his door even before knocking. Starlight sometimes wondered if it was by the use of magic - every fairy had some ability in magic but she and most other fairies never used it, however some, and Starlight was convinced Berberdoff was one of them, could use magic in everyday tasks without thinking about it.

Entering, they saw Berberdoff sitting reading a very large book which was rested on his knees. Looking up at them he asked, "And what can I do for you three?"

"We have all been flying again today," Windfall said, speaking for all three of them. Berberdoff nodded and Windfall continued, "We feel that we have a good escape plan and thought we should be ready to fly out in a few days."

"A few days you say, why not tomorrow?" Berberdoff asked, Starlight was caught off guard by the question. All three of them had discussed the plan but none of them had thought about putting it into action yet.

"Well we thought that if we ran throw it over the next few days we could get it right and be ready to leave early next week." Windfall replied confidently. Berberdoff looked at each of them in turn, Starlight felt as if he was looking deep into her soul. Then, he slowly and carefully put down the large book and pointing in the general directions of some empty comfortable chairs.

"Please come and sit down." The three Fairies went and sat down, Starlight found she was sitting opposite Berberdoff, which she found a bit intimidating, but she found the chair very, very comfortable and could have easily drifted into sleep. After they had settled down, Berberdoff said: "I know you have planned very well for this, so why don't you tell me all about it?"

Windfall began to explain about the flights that she and Starlight had flown at great height looking down and focusing on looking for danger. Dew then explained about her plan for flying at low altitudes but very fast where she could hide on the desert floor until Windfall and Starlight could confirm it was all clear.

Berberdoff listened intently, nodding occasionally but never interrupting. When they had finished speaking he kept nodding slowly to himself, and then asked:

"If you do see danger - how do you communicate that to Dew?" The three girls looked at each other - there was no way but Starlight did not want to confirm this yet.

"That is something we are still working on," said Windfall.

Berberdoff looked at her with a smile: "In other words, you do not have one," he said with a chuckle, and waved away any attempt to reply. He then stood and walked a little way across the room.

"I think you should go," turning he looked directly at Windfall, "I think you should go tomorrow. The more practice you undertake the more likely people are to notice your activities. If people start to notice - you can be sure the creatures which you are trying to escape from will also." Starlight suddenly had the urge to say something but just as she had built up the courage she lost it again. Berberdoff looked at her, as did Dew and Windfall, Berberdoff asked: "You have a question, Starlight?"

"Do you think it really needs to be that quick, and will you tell the Royal Princess?"

"Yes," he said, "and no. I do not think the Royal Princess needs to know, so if, and I hope it does not, but if something does go wrong she can honestly say she knew nothing about it. As I have already said, the longer you three leave it the more likely someone will notice what you are doing. I will say I have been keeping an eye on you from a distance, and from what I have seen I have full confidence in you, but in the end the decision rests with you."

The three girls looked at each other, and then Berberdoff said, "I will leave you three to discuss it for a few moments," he then walked to the other side of the apartment, picking up his book on the way.

Starlight, felt butterflies in her stomach, as she drew close to the others. "Well I'm all for it," said Windfall, looking at the other two, "but I think the decision should really be down to you Dew, you are going to be in the greatest danger."

"I say go, it does not make much difference if we spend more time training, we will not improve any more, and what Berberdoff said is quite true."

"What do you say Starlight?" Windfall asked.

"Go," Starlight replied, excitement replacing the butterflies.

"Very well tomorrow morning at dawn we fly." Windfall said, a wide smile over her face, Starlight saw the same smile reflected in Dew's. Windfall then looked towards Berberdoff and in a louder voice said.

"We fly tomorrow at …," but she was cut off by a hand gesture from Berberdoff.

"Good, I don't need to know details, and if no one else apart from you three know the better. I will wish you luck and will not mention you three to anyone when you have left so I hope no one will notice your absence. Now go and have the best of luck, tell Prince Tagan we need help, but Dew, do not attempt to return with the others, find Princess Megan and stay with her or with Prince Tagan if she is not with the army, You two I hope will be able to get back safely. Now go with my blessing and all my wishes of luck."

The three fairies stood. Starlight did not think she would be able to sleep, the butterflies had returned with a vengeance but it was excitement now, not fear.

None of them spoke as they left Berberdoff's apartment and made their way back to their own. All three fairies lost in their own thoughts which were mixed with fear and excitement!

*****

Faith felt the cool breeze of the Dark Forest brush her face as she stepped out onto the balcony. For the first time she could not remember just how long it had been since she had actually been outside, feeling the slight touch of the wind and hearing the rustle of the leaves in the trees she regretted not making the effort to get out sooner even if it was, like today, just as far as the balcony.

"Are you feeling alright?" the concerned voice of Avtag asked from behind her. Smiling and looking back at her older cousin she said,

"Yes thank you, I was just remembering how long it has been since I have been outside." Avtag, who was her older cousin and the much older brother to Megan, was also the new General to the newly formed Dark Forest Army, which Faith had authorised by the expansion from the old guard. She had to agree in her head that she had been asked several times by Avtag to inspect the growing army, but until now, with the problems from the Star Chamber's unwillingness to support the formation of an army, until her father the King had indicated his willingness for it. Now she could acknowledge the existence of an army of the Dark Forest in the open, and felt a lot better for it, there seemed too much going on behind the scenes!

Looking down at the massed ranks of the green and brown uniformed soldiers she was impressed, she could hardly believe so many could be recruited and trained in such a short time.

"Well I must say General Avtag I am very impressed," Faith heard the deep male voice behind her, and span around to see Chancellor Becket strolling onto the balcony, "how many do they number now, the full five thousand?"

Faith felt a little annoyed that Becket had intruded into what should have been her first chance to see the new army. However with her political head on she was glad that such an important person, other than herself, seemed to be lending support.

"No Chancellor we have only three and a half thousand recruited so far, and about one and a half thousand fully trained," Avtag replied, "but we are working very fast and as hard as we can."

Standing just to the side and behind Faith, Becket said, "Well General, I will say again, I am impressed with all you have achieved, would you agree Royal Princess?" Faith was taken a little off guard, as she was listening to the conversation, but did not think it would involve her. She took her time to reply, something was bothering her about the massed ranks, but could not put her finger on it, something she had seen with all of Tagan's armies but not this one!

"You have no swords or pikes," she suddenly berated when she realised, taking herself off guard.

"No we do not," Avtag replied slowly, "everything we have comes from the forest or the close surrounding area. We have found no iron or copper ore within the Dark Forest so therefore are unable to make swords or tips for pikes, but we do have staffs, spears and plenty of bows and arrows with very sharp flint heads. I think we would be a formable foe for any enemy who entered the Dark Forest!"

"I take it from what you have just said you do not intend to go out and confront the creatures outside the forest?" Becket asked.

"No Chancellor I do not, as far as I'm concerned our job is to defend the Dark Forest, if the creatures enter the Dark Forest we will attack them and I think with all our training in the forest and our knowledge I think we would put up a very good fight. But if we left the forest we would be in open territory and vastly outnumbered, we would be massacred!" Faith saw Becket nodding, with what she took as approval, as he heard Avtag's tactics, she was also impressed.

"Who is doing the training and devising the tactics?" she asked.

"Some of the old guard is doing the training, and I along with my senior officers are thinking up the tactics as we go along, I know they look quite impressive now, I just hope they are as impressive if, or when we are called to fight." He replied, his face looking glum as he finished talking.

"First impressions are very important," Chancellor Becket said with a gentle pat on the General's back, "and my first impression is of a well-trained disciplined army, so you have won the first battle." Avtag gave a slight smile and nod of thanks.

"Could I go down and inspect them, I believe that is the custom in most Kingdoms?" Faith asked, Avtag's face lit up.

"I would be most grateful if you would Royal Princess." So in a short time Faith found herself walking on the forest floor in a large open area where the massed ranks of the army were on parade.

The ranks as she approached stood rigid, it was only as she approached the middle of the front row she realised the ranks were made up of male and female Fairies.

"You have men and women in your ranks, do you intend them all to fight?" Faith asked Avtag as they finished inspecting the front rank.

"With the numbers that we require, a male only army would not provide sufficient numbers. Everyone on parade today, when the time comes, will fight if called upon."

"Well I cannot wait to see the rest of them, will you be joining me Chancellor to complete the inspection, or do you have more pressing duties?" Faith said, Chancellor Becket, who was following, and taking a great deal of interest in the equipment which the soldiers held, smiled.

"I have nothing of greater importance than inspecting our new army with you Royal Princess, and it is also my great pleasure to show my support, after all we do not know what our futures will throw at us."

Faith smiled, and resumed the inspection of the army accompanied by General Avtag and Chancellor Becket, it took quite some time as she and Becket spoke to quite a few of the soldiers within the ranks, so the shadows were beginning to lengthen by the time Faith turned to Avtag in the end and thanked him for such an impressive display. As they left Faith could hear the orders being shouted out for the army to march of. The last time Faith remembered hearing anything similar was when she had been with Tagan and her heart warmed to the thought. She wondered what Tagan was doing at that moment and thought if he would ever have imagined what she had just been doing.

Chapter 11

Where was Megan? Tim was thinking as he walked along the palace corridors in an undignified hurry followed by Stickleback, Colonel Peabody, Major Lord Bazzington and Major Gladstone, behind them were an attachment of the Wildbloods, it was quite an impressive party but hardly noticed as the corridors seemed deserted.

Tim would have waited for Megan, but Stickleback had insisted on them being early, as he had said being late or even punctual would be classed as an insult for a Queen bestowing an honour, even if that honour was, in his opinion outside her authority to bestow.

Stopping outside the very large double doors which opened into the throne room, Tim took a deep breath. He was feeling very nervous, more so than he thought he would, but that was heightened by the feeling of anger, where was Megan?

Two Wildbloods stepped up and opened the doors allowing Tim to look inside the throne room again, the last time he had entered it was to tell of the surrounding of the Dark Forest by the Destroyer's creatures. But he felt shock as he looked in, it was empty! It was almost empty, sitting in the middle of the room on a small chair. Below the platform on which the two thrones should have stood sat Mortimer, his long white hair settling below his waste onto the chair and his long beard hanging between his open knees between his legs.

"Are good you've made it," he said without a hint of irony at the empty room, "I was beginning to get a little concerned."

"Where is everyone?" Tim shouted louder than he had intended, but the shock of not seeing what he had expected to caused his sudden outburst.

"I'm very sorry about that, but there was a last minute change of plan which we did not have time to tell you. I was told to stay here and show you the way to the new venue." Mortimer stood and walked to a door at the far end of the left side of the room, here was another large door. He stopped in front of it allowing time for the two Wildbloods to skirt past him. Mortimer took hold of the two door handles and turned to face Tim and the others.

"Once the doors are fully open, and not before, walk out at a steady pace, it will be obvious where you are to stop, and then just play it by ear." Mortimer said with a slight smirk on his face, "any questions?"

"Have you seen Megan?" Tim asked, and heard an orderable sigh from Stickleback,

"She left very early this morning, with some of her escort," he replied so quietly Tim had to strain to hear, but then continued, "She said she had something to do and something to arrange which she could put off any longer."

The doors had fully opened and the midday sun streamed in causing Tim to blink a few times before he could see, but when he did he was amazed. Both sides of the walk way were lined by the Guardian, inter twined by his new human soldiers of both sexes, all looking very smart in their new, if somewhat strange uniforms, they seemed to have loose fitting robes, with swords hanging loosely from their belts and bows on their backs, he could not tell men from women apart from their height, then further down the line he saw what were clearly women in tight looking one piece body suits, with very small bows hanging from their waist belts and a quiver of arrows from the other. Tim did not ask questions, he would find out in his own time away from public gaze.

Behind these troops, to the left were the Allied Army and to the right, The Mercian Army - all lined up on parade. Beyond them and on stands surrounding the large courtyard were the public who all seemed in a party mood. At the far side of the courtyard where they were heading stood a long platform. The front part was lower and standing at both ends were what Tim took to be ambassadors, from their manner, age and style of dress. There were more of them on the higher rear part of the stage, again at either end. In the middle of the higher stage were two very ornate but empty thrones, the one to the right, slightly more grand and a little forward. On the lower part in the middle was another and either side of this and slightly back were two chairs. One was empty, but the other was occupied by Mortimer. To make up the official party on either side of Mortimer were a further ten chairs, five on each side. From the extremely old looking occupants of these chairs, Tim took them to be the Council of Ten. Tim had never seen them before and he felt he was not alone in that among the population of Kleve.

Tim and his party stopped at the front row of the gathered troops. In front of them a small empty space in the very crowded courtyard. The crowd fell silent in expectation of the next moves in the unfolding ceremony.

As Tim stood and waited he looked around, he was surprised to see some cavalry on the far sides of the standing troops, he had not noticed them before, then his mouth almost fell open, standing beside the mounted cavalry was some type of very hairy humped creature, not mounted but being held by a cavalry soldier.

"What on Earth is that ugly creature?" he gasped, louder than he had anticipated by the turning of heads towards him.

"That is a camel, my Lord," Colonel Peabody replied from behind him.

"Well, thank goodness we don't have any," Tim replied, but turned around when he heard a few coughs and a slight stuffed laugh.

"But we do my Lord," Colonel Peabody said, but before Tim could say anything more movement signalled the start of the ceremony.

To the right, a horned herald lead out the Queen, who was escorted by her husband Prince Sebastian, following them alone was Prince Tagan. He was in turn followed by all the army commanders lead by Lord Avon and Field Marshal Hungerford. It took a short while until everyone was seated and settled.

Mortimer stood up and walked to the lector and with great ceremony began to unroll a scroll. There was a disturbance in the viewing crowd, which Mortimer obviously did not appreciate by the look on his face, Tim found it quite amusing, until he saw Mortimer look up with a look of confusion and then horror, Archers, situated on the roof tops of the courtyard suddenly began to pull back their bow strings with arrows at the ready, the crowd had become quite alarmed and the talk from them increased in volume.

Tim suddenly found two of the largest Wildbloods he had ever seen standing closely either side of him and both looking upwards behind him, turning he realised, apart from the soldiers lined up in their ranks, everyone else was looking into the sky, Tim looked too.

Quite high in the sky were about seven or eight figures, from first glance most of them seemed to be flying Guardian, which would explain the more relaxed posture from the two Wildbloods beside him, Tim thought, but the middle leading figure was different, and for some reason concealed, the figure was in full view, but somehow the features seemed soft, you could not focus on them. Tim then began to feel nervous, this must be magic, he thought, but what magic and who would want to conceal their identity so openly?

Then a gasp from all the onlookers, including Tim as Megan came into full focus, just above his head and flying with her escort to the centre of the space in the courtyard. She looked beautiful Tim thought, with a pure white simple dress, no foot wear that he could see and her hair loose. As she and her escort landed silently she glanced quickly at Tim, giving him what looked like a quick smile and a nod, Tim quickly smiled back, his head full of questions, but events took over.

"May I ask the meaning of your interruption Princess?" Mortimer asked, in a loud firm voice which hardly concealed the rage he felt.

"Your Majesty I beg forgiveness for our interruption, but if I may be so bold I have something of importance to say." Megan then gave the Queen a very low curtsy, holding it at the lowest point until she heard the Queen's voice.

"Please stand Megan," the Queen said, "what is of such importance it takes an entry like that?"

"Before the Champion Lord is changed in any way I must make an announcement." Megan said after she had stood up again. The Queen waved her hand in encouragement for Megan to keep speaking. Megan looked again at Tim and this time she did smile at him, he could see that and he thought she really did look beautiful in the midday sun. Megan then took a deep breath.

"It is a tradition with my people that we should make an announcement, in public for as many to hear of something which will affect our lives and the lives of others, I feel this is such an announcement and a greater number of those who it will affect are here today. I apologise for the interruption Your Majesty, but I feel this is relevant for today." Then Megan gave the Queen another very low curtsy.

"I must say I am intrigued," the Queen replied, "please continue."

Megan, with a slight smile at the Queen's reply, turned towards Tim, her eyes looked to him to be full of fear, which he could not understand but her lips and face gave him the widest smile. Stretching her hands out slightly, she took hold of his, then to Tim's amazement knelt down on one knee. The courtyard fell silent, not even a breath of wind interrupted the scene, and then Megan spoke.

"Timothy Goodbody, I must ask you in front of all these witnesses, if you would honour me by consenting to join me as my life partner, I love you and wish to share that love with you until the day I die." Not a word was murmured as the silence continued as if a spell had descended. No one moved apart from Tim, who gently pulled Megan to her feet, still holding her hands.

"YES, YES, YES," Tim shouted, "I do love you Megan and will be more than honoured to be your husband" Smiling, Megan and Tim embraced as the courtyard erupted into cheers and clapping. Only the Queen and the Royal party looked glum.

After quite an interruption of clapping and cheering the Queen rose to her feet, killing the celebrations almost instantly, Tim immediately saw the worried look return to Megan's eyes as the turned back towards the Queen.

"As romantic and touching as this seems," the Queen said, as the crowd returned to silence again, "I must reminded you Princess Megan, you are not just another Fairy free to live your life as you wish, you have responsibilities to your people which come from your birth, and which you cannot just ignore. I think I am right in saying you are either second, or at the most in line to the throne of the Dark Forest, so in your position you cannot just marry anyone you like, Royal Princesses marry who they need to marry for the good of their people. The consequences for the future are incalculable."

Megan looked down at her feet for a long time, taking deep breaths, Tim thought he saw, but was not sure of a single tear just run down her left cheek, then she squeezed his hand firmly and quickly.

"Your Majesty, I know and understand what you are saying, but you must understand sometimes life is more important than duty, and sometimes our lives become both our duty and honour," the Queen, who was seated again nodded but the sternness was still etched onto her face, as it was to her husband's and Prince Tagan's. "So it is after a great deal of thought and mediation that I have come to this decision, I must follow my heart, I have now known for some time that my destiny lies with the destiny of the Champion Lord. I have fallen head over heels in love with Tim and he makes that destiny all the greater to follow, but I also know what is expected of me in my duty. So I say now for all to hear and report, I renounce all my titles and inheritance, I also renounce any titles and inheritance of any of our children, which may be an entitlement from my blood line - this I say freely and of sound mind."

Silence enclosed the courtyard as Megan finished speaking. Tim gave a squeeze of her hand in encouragement. The Queen did not speak but summoned a Paige to her, following a conversation, which could not be overheard, the

Paige left the queen and quickly walked to where Mortimer was quietly talking to Tagan on the lower stage. They both stopped to hear the message the Paige had bought them, the only reaction Tim could see was a raised eyebrow from Mortimer, then as the Paige left Tagan said a few more unheard words to Mortimer, then he took his seat. Mortimer slowly walked back to the lector and with great ceremony rolled up the scroll which he had been about to read, placing it carefully down he looked out across the courtyard. His gaze eventually falling on Tim and Megan, who stood hand in hand in front of the Guardian and its supporting army.

Mortimer cleared his throat, not to silence anyone - as no one was speaking, but it to make him the centre of attention - a place he liked to be.

"I speak on behalf of and with the authority of Her Majesty, Queen Kathryn of Mercia. Tim and Megan would you please step forward," Mortimer said and as they did, he quickly took the few steps down towards them, greeting them both with a wide smile. "We are here today, now it seems, to join these two young people, Tim and Megan, in matrimony by the ceremony of tying hands, is there anyone who has any just reason in law why these two should not be joined, if so - speak now?" The silence was almost complete, with only the rippling of the flags in the slight wind breaking the spell, but Tim still gave in to the urge to look around to face any challenge. Mortimer bought him back again with his next words.

"Please give me your left hand Megan and Tim if you could place your left hand on top, thank you." He then took a silk ribbon about a foot long and genteelly wrapped it around both their hands, tying it at the end, "This tying of hands is the symbol of the tying of hands is to represent the tying, or joining of hearts. I now declare what has been legally joined may no one try to pull apart, Tim, Megan I now declare you joined as one and pronounce you husband and wife." Tim looked at Megan, the grin on her face matched his own. Mortimer, who was for once also smiling, looked at each of them in turn, "If you wish, I think it is tradition to seal the marriage with a kiss."

Tim slipped his arms around Megan's waist and felt the weight of her arms on his shoulder, but everything slipped into a dream as he felt her warm lips as they kissed. The crowd erupted into loud cheers and clapping. Tim took no notice as he was lost in the warm embrace of Megan.

He did not know how long they kissed but much too soon Tim heard Mortimer say, "We still do have important business to conclude!" Megan broke the kiss to Tim's disappointment, but still held him looking deep into his eyes,

"Now my love, attend to your duties," she said almost as a whisper.

Turning back to Mortimer, Tim slowly untied the ribbon from their hands and tucked it into his belt, Mortimer gave him a stern look at his actions, but said nothing, Megan took hold of his right hand with her left as he bought it back down by his side. Mortimer then picked up the scroll and unwound part of it, looked at Tim and Megan and then beyond them to the armies and crowds gathered in the courtyard.

"Sir Timothy Goodbody, you are also known as The Champion Lord, this is not a title known or for that matter recognized by the Kingdom of Mercia or for that matter any kingdom or nation in this world!" The stirring from the ranks of the Guardian behind Tim made him hope Mortimer would move on, or stop, Tim was unsure if Mortimer knew just how offensive he sounded to the Guardian right then!

"However," Mortimer continued, "it is a title of great significance to our friends and allies the Guardian, so it is for this reason we are gathered here today, to declare from this day forth the title of Champion Lord is recognised and honoured by the Kingdom of Mercia and all the Kingdoms and nations represented here today, it is also to be noted that it is only the Guardian who can bestow this title in whatever method they choose and to whoever and it will still be recognised. Therefore, in conclusion, I on behalf of my Queen and the heads of state all gathered here today say - I recognise and honour you my Champion Lord."

Again, the courtyard was filled with cheers and clapping, but this time the Queen, followed by the entire dignitaries of the nation's rose to their feet clapping.

Tim felt Megan squeeze his hand as he looked back to the Guardian's, ranks, he could not tell if they were smiling, but they all seemed pleased and the humans in his ranks were smiling and laughing. I now have one joined army, Tim thought to himself, we are ready to face whatever the future has in store for us, a sure safe and determined army!

Chapter 12

The early morning mist was still hanging in the canopy of the forest trees, Starlight thought it was about an hour until day break, she shivered in the stillness. The only movement came very quietly from Windfall and Dew who had spread out the three small bags in which they would carry their effects for the journey, and there were very few of them! The two Fairies were trying to even up the weight of the three bags, but the task seemed more difficult as the time drew closer for departure.

Looking up to the tree canopy Windfall could only see the odd star through the morning mist and lightening sky, this could be double edged, she thought, the mist may hide their departure, but it could also disorientate them.

Crack! They all jumped at the sound of a stick breaking,

"Sorry if I alarmed you," Chancellor Becket said in a hushed voice as he immerged from the shadows, "I just thought I would see you safely off and wish you luck."

"Thank you, Chancellor," Dew said, slowly standing, "but Berberdoff said we should leave unannounced so no one here could be held responsible!" Starlight also stood up, her heart just about seemed to be gaining a regular beat again after the shock of the interruption.

"And quite right too," the Chancellor replied, "but as I am normally up at this time, I like to walk in the stillness of the Dark Wood, it helps clear my mind, gets things into perspective, and I just happened to notice you."

"Well again thank you Chancellor, we will try to do our best," Dew said.

"We could not ask for anything more," the Chancellor said, "And just remember what you are doing is very, very important, we need Prince Tagan and his army here now more than ever." He looked as if he was just about to leave when Windfall asked,

"Do you think Chancellor that the Dark Forest is really in danger from those creatures?"

"I do not know with any certainty," the Chancellor said as he stopped and slowly turned around, "but what I do know is those creatures are here, and therefore it is reasonable to assume they are here for a reason, can you think of any other reason why they would be here than to attack us?" Shrugging his shoulders he turned and left the three Fairies standing in silence.

"Well," Starlight was the first to speak, "it's getting lighter, the mist seems to be lifting and we can see to fly to the canopy, I think it is as good a time as ever to go, shall we?" With a nod from the other two the three Fairies picked up their bags and strapped them to their waist. Starlight checked the security of her bag to ensure it would not hinder her, then spreading her wings she flapped them a few times, blowing up leaves from the forest floor. As she flapped a little harder Starlight's feet lifted ever so slightly from the ground. Both Dew and Windfall did the same - Windfall, like Starlight, had the same outcome, but Dew's wings filled the silence with a buzzing sound and she took off, flying up into the canopy. Dew returned to the others after checking the sky above the tree cover.

"It is clear out there, but it is very cold and I could see no clouds." This report was very important for the other two Fairies, they both needed thermals, warm columns of air rising from the ground, the combination of cold air and the lack of clouds could indicate that the early morning sun had not had the time to heat the ground to build thermals, this would not stop Starlight and Windfall flying, but it would take a great deal more effort, on the very day they wanted to cover the furthest distance.

"There is no time like the present," Starlight said to no one in particular, then with outstretched wings she began to beat them in a deliberate manor as she ran along the short clearing under the forest canopy. Soon, very soon she was running in the air as her feet lifted from the ground, a few hard beats of her wings and Starlight shot up towards the overhanging canopy. Quickly searching for the gap which she knew was open, she broke through into the cold early morning sky. Beating her wings with ever greater force, she struggled to gain height, the cold air stung her throat as she gulped air into her lungs, desperately fighting to remain airborne, checking her position she turned west away from the blood-coloured rising sun.

Looking back, she saw Dew, quickly followed by Windfall breaking into the gathering sunlight. Dew shot to the edge of the canopy then dropped out of sight, Starlight felt a lump in her throat until she saw Dew speeding just above the desert floor, throwing a dust cloud in her wake.

"This is more difficult than I imagined it would be," Windfall gasped between beating wings, as she drew level with Starlight, Starlight smiled at her despite the pain in her lungs.

"Well we are here now, and there is no turning back!" The two Fairies together flew in unison out over the desert, suddenly and alarmingly loosing height as they left the safety of the Dark Forest.

Working their wings furiously they very slowly began to gain height. Not a word passed between them as they each concentrated on the rhythm of their beating wings cutting through the cold morning air. The sweat ran down Starlight's face from the intense effort and she could feel the cold air on the dampness of her sweat covered back. Slowly, the chill on her back began to subside as she felt the warm kiss of sunlight. Looking down Starlight could just make out the slight outline of her shadow which could mean only one thing - the sun was now high in the sky. As the realisation dawned on her, Windfall suddenly shot up, turning tightly in an unseen column of rising air but before Starlight could react, Windfall was souring high above her. Not wishing to turn back Starlight began to search out the rising columns of air which she knew would now be created by the sun heating the desert floor.

Whoosh! She suddenly shot up as if an unseen hand had cupped her and lifted her up, turning sharply she opened her wings fully for gliding as she too felt the full advantage of the thermal. Soon she was looking down at the quickly vanishing desert floor.

She broke out of the column of rising air at the top, several thousands of feet up, looking around as she glided to get her bearing she could see Windfall, just higher than her and a short way back.

Looking down, she was still amazed at just how good her eyesight was from this height, she imagined it was the same for all of them, she had just not thought of it before now. Then movement caught her eye, concentrating on a small spot, she inadvertently held her breath. Far, far below her she could just see a still figure, lying down, seemingly lifeless.

"Is that Dew we can see?" Windfall said between breaths, "She seems very still!"

"I think it is," Starlight replied slowly, as she assessed the situation, "We must go down and see if she is alright, but keep a sharp eye open for any danger." Without waiting for a reply she began to lose height, She saw Windfall doing likewise but some distance away.

Soon Starlight was low enough to see Dew in detail, she was lying down, either asleep, or worse, but Starlight cold not see anything to make her sense danger. From her right Starlight saw Windfall fly past Dew - low and slow and then she turned back and landed. By the time Starlight was back on terra firma Dew was awake and apologising to Windfall profusely.

"I'm sorry I was just so tired I thought I would just have a rest, I must have fallen asleep." Dew was saying again and again, Windfall was not replying, letting Dew ramble on, but the slight smile which Windfall was desperately trying to supress, gave her true feelings away. Starlight landed beside them both,

"There is no harm done, and I could see no danger as I landed, so it seems a good time to have a rest and see where we are." The three Fairies sat down, shared some rations and talked about their progress so far, they agreed everything seemed to be going well, in fact better than they had hoped, but it was only the start of the journey and they must not relax.

"When do you think we should start off again?" Dew asked, Windfall was the first to reply,

"That is rather up to how you are feeling Dew? I think we are out of immediate danger now, so you may be able to fly higher and slower now to save your energy."

"Yes," Dew agreed, "it was a rather mad dash, now maybe we can enjoy flying again."

Starlight stood up, arranged and checked her bags which she had hanging from a belt and spread her wings, she saw Windfall and Dew doing the same, then looking up to a nearly cloudless sky she took a deep breath. This was the first time she would be able to take off in a straight line, and not fight for height, avoiding trees. With a smile on her face and a quick glance back to check and see if the other two were ready, she began her take off run. Flapping her wings with purpose, she soon found her feet running in mid-air, her outstretched toes just missing the ground rushing passed her feet, she lifted her legs, and immediately soured higher. Looking back she saw the other two also taking to the air, Windfall the same way she had and Dew just straight up, and very soon Starlight was in the unusual position of looking up at Dew as she changed to level flight.

Starlight slowly gained height in wide circles, enjoying the relaxing air and warm sun on her back. Soon Windfall joined her in the loose open circle which they now flew around Dew, each rotation taking them westward. If this was how they could complete their journey it would be no hardship whatsoever Starlight thought to herself as she enjoyed the relaxed atmosphere.

Movement! Straining her eyes in the steep turn into which she had flung herself to get a better look. Far off in the distance, but moving very fast in their direction, becoming larger and more viable with every passing moment at least a dozen small spots. There was no doubt in Starlight's mind, these were creatures coming to get them.

"Look out we have company," Starlight shouted, "Dew, you dive down and try to fly fast as you can! Windfall, we'll gain height quickly and see what we can then do. I think we may have to fight somehow!"

There was no reply but Starlight saw the two other fairies immediately change their height and do as they were requested. Starlight did likewise and with a few hard flaps of her wings soared.

"Do you have any suggestions of what to do now?" She heard Windfall call to her from slightly above. Looking down from over a thousand foot Starlight could now clearly see the twelve flying creatures, they had made no variation to their flight and were heading straight towards Dew, who was now making good speed, but still the distance was closing. Starlight knew she and Windfall could not match either Dew or the creatures for flat out speed, but she had an idea.

"Follow behind me and do what I do, I have an idea, and I hope it will work," with that Starlight dipped her wing and then drew them in to cause her to dive. The wind rushed passed her ears making a sound almost like a scream. Her eyes watered and then as she gained speed she could feel tears running across her cheeks. The creatures appeared larger and were getting ever closer with every rapidly passing second. Starlight could now see the creatures in all their detail but had to select a target. They were flying so fast and close to the ground the dust was being sucked up in their wake and that was when she had her idea!

Selecting the last creature, she closed her dive in on it, amazed that none of them had noticed her rapid assault. She opened her wings with a load crack and swinging her legs down in front of her she struck the last creature between the wings on its back, with both feet. Desperately flapping her wings in a struggle to gain height she looked down to see her target cartwheel into the desert floor in a crumpled heap - no movement. The rear most creatures were looking around in confusion to see what had happened. Suddenly there was a rush of air and with an ear-piercing crack of air, Windfall targeted the next creature. It hit the ground with such force the ground appeared to shudder. As Windfall began fighting for height again, there was no doubt in Starlight's mind that they must have severely hurt the creatures.

Looking down from her vantage point Starlight realised that they had caused confusion at the rear of the group of creatures. They were now alert and looking for the next attack. The front of the group, however, seemed unaware of the attack and was rapidly gaining on Dew.

Seeing Windfall back up with Dew, Starlight said, "I'm going for the lead one," then not waiting for a reply dipped and dived. The wind screamed passed her ears and the tears streamed from her eyes, but this time she knew what to do and concentrated on her target. Faster and faster she dived, hopping none of the creatures would glance up to see her rapid attack. Larger and larger the creatures appeared as she advanced in on them. She could now see Dew was struggling to maintain her speed. The creatures were gaining on her with every moment and then, wings out – CRACK - legs down - THUD, the creature fell out of the sky. Fighting with every breath to flap her wings and struggling to gain height Starlight fought to exit the danger zone.

CRACK! Starlight turned in shock to see Windfall kick the second creature earthward in a great spiral of sand rock and dust the creature plummeted to its death.

Having gained height Starlight looked back down at their handiwork, Dew had some clear distance now from the creatures that were looking all around them for the source of danger, because of this they had slowed slightly, giving Dew a better chance. Windfall drew up beside Starlight.

"I think we have gained time, but I don't think we have stopped them," Windfall said, "soon they will work out how to defend themselves."

"Yes, but until that time we may as well take advantage of the situation," Starlight said, "would you like to lead this time?"

Windfall smiled, then dived. Starlight watched as she gained speed, then she saw a slight vapour trail from her wingtips, then Starlight judged it was her turn and she dipped and dived. The wind rushed passed her ears, her eyes streaming with tears again. As Starlight followed Windfall in the attack, she chose a target, not the creature behind Windfall's target, which was leading the chase, but two back, she thought that would take them by more of a surprise.

CRACK, Windfall opened her wings. Starlight did not have time to look at Windfall. CRACK, she opened her wings, swung her legs forward, THUD, the creature catapulted out of control hitting the ground hard with such an impact it sent the creature spiralling along the floor like a bag of old bones!

Gaining height Starlight re-joined Windfall, "They are turning back," she said as Starlight drew close, "look we have beaten them!" Starlight looked down, the creatures were turning and flying back, as quickly as they had been chasing Dew.

"I'm going down to tell Dew she can slow down a bit," Starlight said.

"Alright, I will descend a little but will maintain top cover," Windfall replied.

Dropping down to just a few hundred feet above Dew, Starlight called to her that the attack was over, Dew slowed a little and looked behind her, then up to Starlight. Very soon she was in formation with Starlight with Windfall flying above them but close enough to be able to maintain communication without shouting.

They kept a steady pace until the shadows began to lengthen and then they began to look for a place to spend the night. Once settled tiredness soon seeped into their bodies and they slept soundly.

Chapter 13

Tagan walked along the corridor of the palace towards the war room. In the early evening there seemed to be a buzz about, not only the palace, but the whole city. Tagan had walked through the large army camps that now surrounded Kleve, the excitement was static, a rumour had started about a week ago that the army was at last moving, this was reinforced when all the engineers, who were made up of craftsmen and formed into a regiment had left, being escorted by the Greater Longmans Army, under the command of General Flintlock, a very capable and professional army which Tagan had wished would be used in the fight, but that was another question on which his opinion had not been asked.

Arriving at the large and very impressive wooden doors of the war room, Tagan saw more people than were usual for this part of the palace, offices of every rank, most saluted Tagan, to which he nodded a reply, a few of the officers which he knew better, he exchanged a few words with.

"Tagan, I hoped to catch you," a voice he immediately recognised as his brother-in-law Prince Sebastian.

"Sebastian, how are you," Tagan replied as he turned around, "why are you waiting outside with everyone else, why aren't you with my sister?"

"Kathryn isn't coming for the briefing, we had a very detailed and long one yesterday afternoon by Lord Avon, Lord Cogan and Field Marshal Hungerford, I take it you were not informed of it?" Sebastian looked at Tagan in a questioning way, but continued before Tagan could speak, "She asked a lot of question and I think impressed her Generals with her understanding, but thought her being here today may be a bit of a distraction, so I have come to represent her, and if the truth be told, I'm hoping to be given a small command!"

"Do you really think that likely?" Tagan asked as they entered the war room through the large open doors. Inside the room the noise from talking had diminished a little as people found their seats. Tagan looked around the war room with eyes that took in all the familiar surroundings and some new additions. Tagan's seat was in the middle of the front row, Sebastian sat beside him, not in his usual seat which was on the left side of the stage, two seats stood alone, for the Queen and Prince giving the an uninterrupted view of the stage with maps and plans, and the audience sited in a teared semi- circle, giving each an uninterrupted view. Behind Tagan sat all his commanders from Generals to Colonels and their aids, the seat to Tagan's right was empty, and no one seemed in a hurry to occupy it. The rest of the front row was taken up by the four different armies represented, the Mercian home army, who would stay behind to defend Mercia if they were not successful. The deployable Mercian army, which was led by Lord Cogan and going and fight alongside the Allied Army.

To the far left, furthest away from where Tagan sat was Tim, and beside him Megan still looking as radiant as a new bride can, the other side of Tim was Stickleback and behind them the commanders of the Guardian Army, both human and Guardian.

Tagan heard the huffing and puffing well before he saw the course, but he knew the reason, Mortimer was making his way through the crowd of people, making it quite clear of what he thought of them not making way for him, Mortimer always had an over inflated opinion of his importance, Tagan thought to himself with a smile.

"If this is the organisation of the Army I have very little hope of us ever reaching the other side of the desert!" he exclaimed to all that could hear if they wanted to or not.

"Hello Mortimer, how are you today?" Tagan asked with a wide smile as Mortimer took his seat, a scowling look did not encourage a reply.

Very soon all who had seats were seated. There were a few of the more junior aids standing, just inside the doorway or at the side of the walkways. They were trying to keep out of the way of people while still looking as if they were meant to be there.

The room fell silent as the occupants saw the three men walking in through a small door to the right. They were, in Tagan's opinion, the three best military tacticians he had known. Lord Cogan entered the room and was followed by Lord Avon and the small, seemingly insignificant, figure of Field Marshal Hungerford., however it was Field Marshall Hungerford who all-knowing eyes were on.

Lord Cogan sat in the front row with his commanders and officers of the Mercian Army, Lord Avon and the Field Marshal mounted the small stage and sat on two chairs in the middle of it, just to the left of them was a small platform with a lectern to its left, normally this was in in front of the platform for the briefing officer to read notes from, but Tagan imagined it had been moved so Sylvester could talk from it, and not be hidden. On the wall to the right was a large map showing in quite a lot of detail the intended route of the march.

The silence in the room, only interrupted by the odd nervous cough, grew, if possible even more intense as Lord Avon stood and took the few steps to the platform. Arranging a few papers on the lectern then turned to face the room, looking like a stern headmaster he seemed to take every inch of the room in, scanning every detail until satisfied.

"Ladies and Gentlemen," he began with a deep clear voice, "you are all about to set out on properly the greatest quest in all our lives, and I wish you well, but before I hand over to Field Marshal Hungerford to brief you on the plan I wish to announce the new command stricter decided on by the Queen yesterday." A low murmur broke out across the room, and Tagan give Sebastian a quick glance, but the expression on his face showed he didn't know what was to come. "Field Marshal Hungerford is to be removed from his post as Deputy Commander of the Allied Army and is now Supreme Commander of the Expeditionary Forces." Now the murmur grew louder as Lord Avon, with a smile, picked up his papers and walked back to his seat. He gave Sylvester a quick nod and sat down - Sylvester did not stand immediately, but sat looking out over the room, until silence returned.

Leaning over to Tagan, Sebastian whispered, "Did you know anything about this?"

"No, it's all new to me," Tagan whispered back, "but it does make perfect sense, and if you think of it, there is now a command position I need to fill, if the Queen is in agreement of course?" Sebastian gave him a worried smile and sat up.

Silence had descended onto the room as Sylvester got down from his seat and walked slowly to the small platform. He had no notes to refer to, so stood looking out across the room, a pin dropping would have made a shattering sound the silence was so intense, such a small man in size inspired such respect.

When he spoke, his words seemed calm and reassuring. He thanked everyone for all their hard work so far and asked they pass his thanks on to their troops. He then began to outline the plan in detail, pausing and asking individuals who were directly involved if they understood. He answered questions in detail, never having to refer to any notes or consult anyone. It was a performance to inspire trust and it succeeded. He outlined how a mule railway was being constructed across the desert as they marched, to speed up the resupply of everything from food and water to replacement uniforms and weapons. How stages forts would be set up so if the line was broken the supplies were never at the far end of a vulnerable chain, how an army were already deployed to guard the route and informed every one of the newly formed support troops.

Tagan was impressed as he listened, taking relevant notes, as everyone irrespective of rank or position did likewise. The hours of the briefing seemed to fly and then Sylvester said, "Well it only leaves me to wish you all the best of luck in our great adventure, I know, and I will be totally honest in telling you that this is a trap in which we are walking into. But the best way of defeating a trap is springing it on your own terms, and that is what we intend to do. The odds are against us, but with our fighting spirit and esprit de corps I am confident we will win through. A pack of a brief outline of the plan and a more detailed explanation of each of your responsibilities has been sent to you for after this briefing. Well again good luck, we march at drawn."

As Sylvester stepped down from the platform, and then accompanied by Lord Avon out of the door as the room exploded into a great cheer and clapping.

As the room began to clear, Tagan remained seated, he noticed Sebastian and Mortimer did likewise, and then Sebastian turned to him and said, "Did you honestly not know that your second in command is now going to be your commander?"

"No, I honestly did not know that," Tagan replied, "but it seems the right decision as Sebastian has made the plan and he is a lot better at that type of thing, but I do not think he will have made the battle plan, he will leave that to the commanders of the armies at the time, that is why Sylvester is so good, he knows what he is good at and leaves what others are better at a free hand to get on with it, did you not know anything about it?"

"No," Sebastian said, "it was not mentioned yesterday at any point, but I assume as Lord Avon said it that the Queen knew and approved!"

"Well shall we go and ask her," Tagan said, "I haven't spoken to my sister for a few days and I think I should before

I leave. We could ask her about taking that vacancy I suddenly have to fill. Are you coming to see the Queen Mortimer?"

Mortimer suddenly looked up, surprised to be spoken to as he seemed lost in deep thought, "Augh no, sorry, it seems too much of a family affair and if we leave tomorrow I have a few last minute things to do and people to see."

With that he stood and left the rapidly empting room, Tagan and Sebastian waited a moment longer then left towards the royal quarters of the palace.

The guards on the entrance to the royal corridors was not the only signal that you had entered another part of the palace, the floor and wall hangings became noticeably grander, and the lighting increased to illuminate them. Here also servants in royal livery could be seen hurrying along the corridors, stopping only to give Tagan and Sebastian a quick bow or curtsy before hurrying along on their tasks.

They arrived at the grandly decorated large double doors of the royal apartment, four guards stood here, one each side of the door and two on the wall opposite, they saluted the two princes but did not attempt to block their way. Sebastian opened one of the doors and entered without knocking, holding it so as it did not slam shut on Tagan.

Tagan saw that his sister Queen Kathryn had been alone in the room sitting on a very large settee. Sebastian immediately went across to her and kissed her, then sat down on an empty chair next to her, Tagan went across to her,

"Well I must say my long lost younger brother has come to see me, what have I done to deserve such an honour?" Tagan kissed her on the cheek.

"Sorry Kathryn but I have been very busy and at the most I haven't seen you for a few days." He said before sitting down himself.

The Queen then turned to her husband and asked, "And how did the briefing go, did you learn anything new from what we were told yesterday?"

"Well yes I did actually," Sebastian replied with a smile, "We learnt that Field Marshal Hungerford has now been promoted to supreme commander, when did you decided that?"

Kathryn smiled back at Sabastian, but before replying indicated to a servant who was standing at the side of the room for wine to be bought for everyone, then said,

"Yesterday evening, Lord Avon asked for a private audience and proposed it then, his reasoning was very good and in my opinion the Field Marshal is one of the most capable military leaders I have ever meet, why do you have a problem with it?"

"No, no my dear, but did you not think of telling Tagan, after all he was his boss, and now he is working for him!"

The Queen looked down a little, thinking then looked at Tagan. "I'm sorry Tagan, I did not think, but now I see I have put you in a difficult position. I hope you can accept my apology?"

"You have nothing to apologise for," Tagan said, "it was the right decision and one properly if anything, should have been made sooner." The Queen nodded her thanks, but then Tagan continued, "The only problem I have now is finding at such short notice a capable replacement for my second in command one who I know has the experience and who I can trust, which is going to be hard as everyone I would have liked from within the army already has an important job!"

"Well," the Queen said, "this is such an important expedition as Lord Avon pointed out, you have my blessing to look anywhere for a replacement. Who would you have in mind?"

"I don't think you'll like it," Tagan said slowly, "but the most reliable person who I know, who I can trust and I know has a wealth of military experience and in command is Sebastian."

The Queen looked shocked, her face turning quickly between Tagan and Sebastian.

"What - Sebastian? My Sebastian? My husband? You want Prince Sebastian to be your second in command?" Her voice was rising with every statement. Tagan looked calm, but a slight smirk played on his lips as he saw his sister's predicament. She did not want her husband to go, that would be normal for any wife, but at the same time to say no would be an insult to her husband but to say yes would be an insult as the Queen's husband should be in charge, and not the second in command to her brother! Tagan did not, well not too much, like to see the situation in which he had placed her, and could understand all her reasons. At the same time, Sebastian was, from Tagan's point of view, a perfect choice.

Sebastian himself had a sick, off colour look on his face. After a silence that to Tagan seemed to go on an eternity, the Queen said, "I'm sorry my dear, but Tagan's question came out of nowhere, it is you who are important, what do you want to do?"

"Well," Sebastian said slowly, "this is the greatest danger our kingdom, or indeed the world has ever faced. So far I have sat back and watched Tagan and the others face it without lifting even a finger myself, I do feel that at such a time of crises I should be playing my full part."

The Queen with a smile to her husband nodded, then after a deep breath said. "I quite understand and yes agree, but you are my Husband a Prince of Mercia and therefore should have a command and not be subordinate to anyone. If you wish to go I feel you should be in command of the Allied Army and Tagan your deputy!"

Tagan's mouth fell open, but before he could speak Sebastian said, "Sorry my dear, but that would never do, Tagan is their commander. I know Mercia supplies troops to the Allied Army, but so do many other countries. It is as much up to them as us who commands them and they have appointed Tagan. You also know he is about the best field commander Mercia has and I would see it as a great honour to serve both you and the Allied Army as its deputy commander."

Tagan did not realise he had been holding his breath as Sebastian had spoken, but now he let it go. The Queen was smiling at Sebastian, but spoke to Tagan.

"My dear brother, come and give your sister a kiss goodbye, I wish you well and I do have confidence in you. Go and defeat the curse of this Destroyer and save Faith - who I do know you have feelings for." Tagan walked over and gave his sister a kiss and a cuddle. Before he stood up again, his sister whispered into his ear, "Now please leave us as I only have one night to say good bye to my husband and get him ready to go to war!"

Chapter 14

The night was waning and the air thick with candle smoke as he leaned back and rubbed his sore eyes. Colonel Peabody had been reading and writing last minute reports all night, meeting with his deputy Major Gladstone to check everything had been completed and then being joined for a briefing by Captain Summerbee, the Scout leader, whose responsibilities had expanded greatly. She now not only had scouts on camels but also flying on the backs of Griffins.

Peabody looked at the pile of reports stacked on the table before him, had he missed anything? Looking out of the window he could see the eastern sky greying showing time was slipping past. His regiment would be one of the first ones marching along with the Guardian under the command of the Champion Lord. His feelings were a mixture of pride, honour and worry, worry in case he had forgotten something important, and now he would get no sleep. He heard the door open behind him but did not look, he could do without another report to read.

"URCH!" Peabody nearly jumped out of his skin as he felt hands on his shoulders around his neck,

"Have you had any sleep yet?" He heard the soothing voice of Willow ask as she rubbed his shoulders and neck, it felt good and relaxing.

"No, and there seems no point now it's nearly dawn and we will be leaving." Peabody replied, closing his eyes to the feel of her hands soothing away the tension in his neck he did not realise he had, "and I had a lot of last minute things to catch up on before we set out, after all I do not want to let the Champion Lord down!"

"I do not think the Champion Lord would be best pleased if you fell off your horse because you were asleep and broke your neck, you are the commander of one of his regiments and you should have given this task to other people to check - you should be getting told everything is well after you have had a good night's sleep!" His head slumped to the side as she rubbed his neck, "I hope you're not falling asleep now, it's too late," she said.

"No," he said, "I was just enjoying the relaxing feeling."

"Well you'd better stop relaxing and get ready, your army is already lining up to march, and you should have relaxed last night in bed asleep!" With a quick squeeze of the back of his neck she set about collecting all the documentation and putting them neatly into a saddle bag.

Peabody rubbed his head again and stood. He looked at Willow but did not say anything. She would not like work to be interrupted. Walking outside he was shocked to see just how light it was. Peabody could see the dawn was racing along as the outline of grey clouds began to become visible on the eastern horizon.

Peabody made his way towards his living quarters. A quick cold wash would shake the feeling of sleep from him. Just as he came to the door he saw Stickleback striding along, accompanied by a gaggle of his aids. He was firing off orders which an aid would then scurry away to carry out. As the last aid left, on his particular task, Peabody saw Stickleback come to an abrupt halt as he saw Peabody.

"Good grief man, you look terrible, even for a human!" Stickleback exclaimed, "Have you been awake all night?"

"Yes," Peabody called back without adding any further explanation.

"The Champion Lord wants to see us all in about ten minutes, I'll tell him you will be a few minutes late."

Without reply, Peabody hurried into his room, his few possessions were already packed and mostly gone. He quickly found a bowl and jug of water, now cold, but he knew it would have been piping hot when it had been put out, but now cold was good, he needed refreshing and wakening.

The door opened behind him. This seemed to be happening a lot recently and he heard bags being picked up. "Sorry to disturb you Sir, but I'm just picking up the last of your things that need to go." It was Peabody's manservant Dobley, Peabody was still getting used to the idea, but he had been told as a person in his position he should now have a manservant, "I have also laid out a new uniform on your bed for you Sir."

"Thank you," Peabody replied as he splashed water on his face. Walking into his bedroom, as he dried himself, he saw his uniform neatly laid on his bed. Wishing momentarily he could slip into bed for a much longed for sleep he began to undress and then pull his clean uniform on, it looked pressed and smelt clean and fresh. Shortly after buckling his sword belt around his waist and adjusting it for comfort he looked at himself in three quarter length mirror. The reflection that looked back at him was of a confident senior office in a very impressive, if understated uniform, but one that radiated authority. Peabody was pleased with the result, and left his room to attend the meeting with a fresh spring in his step.

He walked across the flying field, here the day's work had already started, at very first light Peabody knew an air patrol had been sent up to check the surrounding area of Kleve. A Griffin with three people on its back to make up the crew, an observer, which was a woman trooper of his Air Bourn Scouting unit and two very small Troggs with bows and arrows which each sat in a light wicker basket each side of the Griffin just behind its wings. The Observer sat on the

Griffin's neck just behind its head and in front of its wings, a woman trooper was the best solution as she was a volunteer and chosen if she was of a small stature and light in weight. This way the observer could mark on maps the enemies' location and strength, and the Troggs could help defend the Griffin from attack, everything had worked very well so far in training, but soon they would be in action for the first time against a ruthless enemy!

Peabody knew all of this information as the Air Bourn Scouting unit was part of his expanded command as was the Long Range Desert Group, who were now trained to make extended scouting trips and if possible raiding parties into the desert to disrupt and gain information on the enemy, both units were made up of volunteers, and both were oversubscribed!

Leaving the flying field he walked down a long open path, here most of his army was lining up in columns ready to march. Most of the soldiers, who noticed him as he passed, nodded and muttered an acknowledgement, with all the officers saluting - which he returned. Passing the rows of the Guardian he noticed most seemed to be asleep, but still standing and lined up in their columns which was a strange and eerie sight.

At the head of the long column was a small group of the armies most senior officers, he knew them all including the Guardians and standing in the centre stood the

Champion Lord, this time unusually not accompanied by his new wife, the Lady Champion.

"I am sorry I am late my Lord Champion." Peabody said as he joined the group, the Champion Lord immediately stooped talking to Stickleback and turned towards Peabody, his heart sank at the rebuke he was expecting.

"My dear Colonel," the Champion Lord said, his youthful face reflecting his enthusiasm which seems to be contagious throughout his entire army, "you are not late, we were just having a chat before we started the formal stuff, I do not even know if everyone who should be here has arrived yet?"

"All of your command who should be here are, Sir." Peabody heard whispered in his ear. Turning around he saw Major Lord Bazzington, who had spoken and next to him Major Gladstone, his two most senior officers just behind them were Captain Summerbee, the Scout leader, and Titus, a fairy with a lot of experience in air recognitions so was now in charge of the Air Bourn Scouting unit. He felt slightly embarrassed as he had been the last of his command to arrive.

"I believe all my command is also here, My Lord Champion." Stickleback said, having obviously over heard what had been said to Peabody. The Champion Lord, looked around at the gathered officers, as if deciding on what to say, he then seemed to gather his thoughts.

"I am not going to make a speech, or give any last minute orders, I think the Field Marshal covered just about everything that needed to be said yesterday. I have nothing really to add other than I thank you all for all your hard work up to this point. Please pass my sincere thanks on to your troops. All the hard work is now going to be put to use. We are the vanguard of this expedition which, have no illusions, is going to be very hard. I expect our army to do all that is asked of it and more to complete this task, but at the same time I do not want any waste of life and expect to bring as many of our troops back as possible. Now good luck to you all - we will be moving out very shortly."

Peabody turned to his commanders, "Well Lady and Gentlemen let us get to it and mount up," he returned the salutes as they all turned to their appointed place, "Titus," Peabody called, Titus stopped.

"Yes Sir," he said.

"Your Air Wing does not move out today, is that correct?" Peabody asked.

"Yes, Sir we will stay here until we have an established landing ground, but we will be providing top cover and reconnaissance," Titus said.

"Very glad to hear it," Peabody said, "well good luck to all your flyers."

Peabody walked back to his position at the head of his regiment, the main body of his regiment was lined up behind the Guardian, as they marched faster, but come the desert many of his troops would fan out, scouting the way ahead.

Seeing his horse with its rains being held by Willow who was already mounted, she gave him a slight smile as she handed him his rains. Mounting with little effort he looked back at his regiment, it looked a strange assortment. A company of light cavalry on horseback leading, they were followed by two companies of infantry and archers marching on foot, which were followed by two companies of cavalry on camels. At the rear of his regiment was the Long Range Desert Group, also on camels. When they had cleared the forests and reached the desert these would fan out and scout in front of the entire army.

There was no order so far as Peabody could hear, the army just started to move forward. No bugles sounded and so far as he could see no one waving them off, which suited his mood. This was a necessary campaign, not a glorious adventure!

The sun glimpsed over the eastern horizon, giving the first hints of warmth, and brightening Peabody's mood, it's amazing how a little warm sunshine can brighten everything up, he thought to himself.

"Would you care to share what is amusing you?" Willow asked, he had not realised she had taken up position by his side, "you are grinning like a Cheshire cat!"

"I was just thinking how ironic it is that a little warm sun can make the entire world seem better," he replied looking at her, the smile still on his face, "but very soon when we are in the desert we will be cursing that same sun!"

Willow did not reply, and Peabody did not expect her to, she was probably trying to strike up a light hearted conversation to pass the time, but he still had all the nights work running around in his head, he could tell he was not good company this morning, but he knew his mood would brighten now they had started the campaign.

Chapter 15

The fingers of sunlight edged over the eastern horizon, announcing the end of a very cold night, although the warmth had still to filter through, Starlight knew it would not take long before the three of them would be wishing for the cool night air again.

She stretched under her blanket, as she tried to build up the inclination to rise from her slumber. Becoming more aware of her surroundings she could make out low words being spoken, and some crackling, almost as if something was on fire, then a smell reached her nostril's, the smell of something reassuring and homely. But they were in the middle of the desert! Panic set in as she rolled over and leapt up, wings open and ready to fly at an instant!

"Good morning, sorry didn't intend to disturb you," Dew said sitting by a fire with some type of animal cooking on it, Windfall sat the other side of the fire, "But as you're awake, you might as well have something hot to drink, last night was very cold."

Starlight struggled to get up, the ground was very hard, and the coldness of the night seemed to have seeped into every muscle she had, making her feel very stiff. Walking over to join the other two at the fire she could feel the radiated heat washing over her cold body and the smell of the cooking meat was making her stomach rumble as she remembered just how hungry she was.

"Here drink this," Windfall said handing her a wooden cup, "be careful it is very hot but will help warm you up, the meat should be ready soon." Thanking her Starlight took the cup, and before drinking, sat down in between the other two, then she lifted the wooden cup to her lips. The drink had a sweet honey taste, she could feel the warmth seeping into her body making her inwardly glow.

After she had begun to feel more like herself, Starlight asked where they had been able to gather the fire wood from and catch something to eat. Windfall said that there was more dead wood around the rocky areas of the desert than she had expected and finding enough wood for a fire was quite easy, then Dew said how she used to go out as a child and hunt with her father in the Dark Wood, and adapting what she knew to the desert was quite simple.

Very soon the meat had finished cooking, and all conversation stopped as they ate. By the time they had finished, the sun was quite high and the heat of the desert was rising.

"I think we should try to cover our campsite as much as possible," Windfall said, "and then today fly as high as we can, it will be cooler for you, Dew, and safer as we will be able to see any danger."

"Do you think we are still in danger?" Dew asked.

"I have no idea, I hope not, but if we go on the plane that we are always in danger, we will be ready for anything," Windfall replied.

After an industrious effort by all three Fairies, they stood back to admire their work. If anyone looked very carefully there was still evidence that the place had been used as a campsite, but a casual glance would reveal nothing. Pleased with their work the fairies arranged their supplies between them and were ready to go.

With no obstructions like trees to avoid, Starlight and Windfall took to the air with ease after a short run up. Dew as normal was able to do a standing start. Very soon the three of them were up in the warm blue sky, Windfall highest by a few hundred feet from Starlight who flew just above Dew. Visibility was a great distance with only the odd fluffy cloud high above them and what looked like the beginning of a slight heat haze below on the horizon.

The flying was effortless, if the landscape was slightly boring, with very few if any features. But they were making good time Starlight thought, and hopefully after a few days they would have completed the desert and into a more interesting landscape of trees, hills, rivers and fields.

"Can you see those black spots on the horizon?" Windfall called down to Starlight and Dew. Starlight looked up at her, then in the direction in which she was pointing.

"No sorry I can't see anything," Starlight said.

"Well, if you flew a little higher you would probably be able to see what I can see!" Windfall replied in a tone which just about covered her sarcasm.

"They are probably birds, but if you really want us to we can turn a little left, that way if they are flying towards us, whatever they are, our paths won't meet." Starlight bit back. They changed course, but there seemed to be an atmosphere surrounding the three Fairies. Starlight was annoyed at being spoken to in such a way by Windfall, who in her opinion seemed to think she was in charge. Apart from that, she had spoiled a nice day. Dew flew close to her and whispered.

"I don't think she is trying to be bossy...."

"LOOK!" Windfall screamed from above, cutting off the rest of Dew's words, "they have changed directions and are heading towards us again!"

With a shake of her head, Starlight said, "I'll go up and see just what she wants!" Climbing beside Windfall, she gave her a cold stare. Windfall did not seem to notice but not taking her eye from the direction in which she was looking, said, "They are not birds, I have counted them. There are about ten, flying in two separate formations and have

173

changed course towards us!" Starlight didn't reply but looked off towards the horizon.

"Oh!" she exclaimed, "They are creatures flying directly towards us - , what shall we do?"

"Let's get down to Dew," Windfall said and immediately dived towards Dew, Starlight followed leavening out beside Dew on the opposite side to Windfall.

Very quickly, Windfall explained the situation to Dew, and then gave the brief outline of a plan. After checking that everyone understood the situation and plan Windfall flapped her wings hard to gain height quickly, Starlight followed her up, higher and higher they climbed with the air getting chillier with the altitude.

Looking down Starlight struggled to see Dew far, far below them, she seemed very low and slow, blending in with the sand below her. Starlight hoped the plan would work, but the way Windfall had explained it, she seemed to have thought of everything.

The creatures continued their unwavering journey towards them, only changing formation as three creatures broke and began to gain height. Starlight felt herself take a deep breath, and hold it as she watched the creatures approach.

Suddenly, the creatures stopped their onward flight towards them and began to circle, short of where the three

Fairies hid in open sight. They were clearly searching for them.

"It looks to be working" Starlight said in a whisper, as she again looked down to where Dew should be, but could see nothing.

"I would not get your hopes up too soon," Windfall replied in just as quieter a whisper. As Windfall spoke, Starlight watched in horror as the lowest flying creatures suddenly changed direction and headed off in a different direction at speed.

"They've seen her!" Gasped Windfall, Starlight looked just ahead of the three lowest creatures and could just see the slight movement of Dew as she gained speed and height in an attempt to out run them.

Without a word Windfall turned into a headlong dive. Starlight watched her for a short time as she gained speed, then turning herself she dived towards the creatures. As she gained speed the wind whizzed past her ears and caused her eyes to water, blurring her vision. Dodging the highest creatures Starlight saw her target, a slow circling creature which appeared to be searching for Dew. From the corner of her eye she could just make out the figure of Windfall just before she attacked her target, but Starlight transferred her vision and concentration back to her own target so she would not miss.

Opening her eyes as wide as she could to clear her vision, she concentrated on the back of the ever growing creature which she was aiming at.

CRACK! The air cut below her open wings, the creature suddenly looked up just as Starlight kicked the creature in the back between its wings with both her feet, sending it hurtling earthwards, out of control. Starlight just looked back to see the creature's broken lifeless body spread on the desert floor. Looking upwards she flapped her wings cutting into the air as she fought to gain height. Dodging the attacking creatures with ease, Starlight followed Windfall for a second attack.

"You go first this time and I'll be right behind you." Windfall said as Starlight drew close. Looking down Starlight saw a trail of dust following Dew as she dashed for safety.

"WAIT!" Windfall called, "Look there is more of them coming, and Dew will never be able to out run them all!" Starlight looked to where Windfall indicated and saw several banks of creatures flying directly towards them in formation of several different heights.

"Dive towards Dew, missing all the creatures and head her off south," Windfall said, "I will take out the lowest one to give Dew a chance, but I think we must change direction away from the way we want to head. It may just give us some space and time. Otherwise, I do not hold out much hope of Dew surviving."

With dread and not answering Windfall, Starlight turned into a steep dive. She had no better ideas so could not argue, but she did not like the thought of turning south, to what she had been told was the hottest part of the entire desert. The alternative seemed clear as she dived towards Dew, eyes streaming and dodging creatures, she would need all the speed she could gain at low altitude as she would be vulnerable to being attacked by the creatures.

THUD! Pain shot through her body, she had not seen the creature with which she has collided. Gathering herself she looked for Dew, seeing her she shot below her, turning sharply in front of Dew she shouted.

"FOLLOW ME!" Without waiting for a reply, Starlight spread her wings and beat them as she flew south. Soon gaining height she felt a little safer she looked down to see Dew following her, but looking up and back she could not see Windfall anywhere, but even better the creatures did not seem to be following them.

The sun was at its height and sweat dripped off Starlight as she decided to gain altitude and take a look at their situation. They had been flying south for what seemed like hours now and had had no further contact with the creatures but also they had had no sighting of Windfall!

Slowly circling Starlight looked down, scanning the empty sky and desert. They were alone, not a sign of any living thing. Scanning the skies Starlight sought for a sign of

Windfall, but nothing, after several more minutes of looking around, Starlight with a heavy hart dropped down towards Dew.

"If you are ready for a break I think we are alone now." Without another word the two Fairies lost height and finding a suitable spot and landed.

Neither Fairy spoke, both consumed in their own thoughts. Starlight felt her eyes wet again, but this time they were tears running down the cheeks on her face, and the knot in her stomach with worry.

Chapter 16

"Enter," Faith responded to the heavy knock on the door, which slowly opened to let Berberdoff into the brightly-lit room.

"Royal Princess," Berberdoff said with a low nod of his head, "I hope I'm not disturbing you?"

"No please come in, sit down and tell my all the news you have, I haven't been updated for what seems like an age." Berberdoff looked around, then took a seat not too far from Faith, whose eyes closely watched as he settled down, then after he seemed to have finished Faith asked, "What news have you bought me, I hope it's all good but please do not spare me from any bad news?"

"Well," Berberdoff began slowly, "I hope I do not have any bad news, but I will tell you what I know and hope it is all good." Faith smiled in response, but did not speak so Berberdoff continued.

"The creatures do not seem to have grown in numbers, but at the same time there is no evidence of the numbers getting fewer. Your Royal Guard is training well, and I must say they are looking very professional, in my humble opinion." Faith nodded in response, she had seen the guard herself recently, and was also impressed, but she had not been told about them being called the Royal Guard, but if that was the most pressing problem she could live with that. She also knew about the state of the creatures and hoped this was conversation before Berberdoff got to the information she was really interested in, she was not disappointed.

"The three girls have left a few days ago and so far it seems no news is good news, I do not know which day they left, but I haven't seen them, or heard anyone speaking about them for several days now."

"Thank you, that was the news I was really waiting for," Faith replied, then after a moment's thought added, "is there anything else you can think of that we can do, I feel so frustrated and inadequate?"

"The only thing we can do is not to provoke the creatures," Berberdoff answered, "we still do not know why they are there or what they want. But I agree Royal Princess, it is frustrating!" Faith nodded but did not speak, her mined was working on the problem.

After a moment she asked, "Have you spoken to Chancellor Becket recently, I wonder what his thoughts are?"

"No, sorry, I haven't seen him neither, would you like me to speak to him about something?" Berberdoff replied. Faith looked at him, a smile spreading across her face as her idea developed, it was so simple why had no one thought of it before?

"You and Chancellor Becket are both diplomates why don't you simply think of what diplomates do best, talk!" Faith said. Berberdoff looked slightly confused.

"Sorry, I don't understand what you are getting at?"

"Why don't we just send someone out to talk to the creatures, ask them what they want here?" Faith exclaimed, her arms outstretched, it seemed so simple! The reaction she received from Berberdoff was not what she expected. She thought he would suddenly see the light and agree, but he did not.

"Royal Princess," he began, his words very deliberate and low, as if he was choosing everyone with care, "from the information we have we do not believe the creatures can talk. They look like lizards but behave most of the time like extremely large insects. We have no idea how, or even if they communicate with each other. I would compare their behaviour to that of a giant swarm of Locusts." Seeing the look of disappointment on Faith's face, Berberdoff quickly added, "But I will speak to the Chancellor and ask him of his opinion as to the question of approaching the creatures to ask what their intensions are." Faith smiled in reply but felt his response was just to humour her.

"Is there anything else you wish to ask me about, Royal Princess?" Berberdoff asked. But Faith replied there was not, and thanked him for his opinion. He then giving a low bow left Faith alone with her thoughts. She was wondering if help was on its way and for that matter if help was in fact needed.

*****

Tagan sat upright upon the back of his new mount Sandy, an ironic name for the chestnut brown mare, but one that appealed to Tagan's sense of humour with the forthcoming campaign. From this viewpoint of a small hillock just outside the tree line Tagan had noticed immediately the intense heat from the still rising sun.

To Tagan's left, a short distance on the next rise was quite an established camp. There were no tents in this camp, every building was made of wood or stone. This was the main base camp. From this camp Tagan could see running out towards the east four cart tracks of wood, separating from each other to quite a distance. These tracks were for heavily loaded carts to be pulled by pack horses or camels, it had been calculated that one horse or camel could easily pull a load along the tracks about twice that without their use.

Each of the separate armies had taken a position along the tracks, using it as a central guide, but never stepping between the rails. Everyone had been warned that the tracks were their life line and must be looked after at all cost!

Thousands of white tents had sprung up as if by magic, but in the middle army fewer tents were visible. These were the Guardians whose insect creatures did not use tents and the elements of the Long Range Desert Group, a recognisance unit who were scouting out the desert well ahead of the remaining armies on their camels already. Just beyond this army the occasional Griffin could be seen taking to the air with their crew of a spotter and two Trogs for defence, occasionally two flying Wildbloods would escort them, knowing what lay over the horizon was essential.

"I thought the last two weeks struggling though the wet undergrowth of the forest was bad, but looking out there I think we will soon be dreaming of the rain," Prince Sebastian said from beside Tagan, but Tagan did not reply, he did agree quietly to himself, but for a commander to voice that opinion was wrong.

The sound of galloping horses made both Tagan and Sebastian turn to look. They saw Field Marshal Sylvester Hungerford, Lord Cogan, The Champion Lord, with Megan at his side and General Flintlock, the commander of the Greater Longmans Army whose role was to protect the other armies and the track, ridding up towards them. As they drew close and stopped Sylvester began to address them.

He told them to pass his thanks onto their troops for such a speedy march so far, but said now the journey had only just began, they would stay where they were for the next two days to bring forward as much of the supplies as they could, and then advance on a bored front so when they did make contact with the Destroyer's creatures they would be ready to fight!

It was not two days, but four days of intense activity, and in those four days the army had changed from working in day light to nights. Surprisingly this had resulted in more supplies being bought up, which Sylvester then decided was of more benefit than moving off. So as evening fell and the heat faded Tagan sat upon his mount watching the armies departing as one, but separated, the distance between the armies would eventually be the equivalent of a day's ride. But all advanced at the same pace.

"Well, this is it, no turning back now!" Tagan said to no one in particular.

"I thought there was no turning back once we had left Kleve?" Sebastian said from his side.

Tagan smiled and looked at him, "Yes, I suppose you're right. It just seems we are now on a collision course of fate, and whatever the outcome is, no one will be untouched."

"But our loved ones will be safe, whoever we are from General to foot soldier that is the essence of what we fight for." Sebastian answered with such a true statement nothing more needed to be said.

Darkness fell quickly, and the night air began to chill, the contrast in temperature between day and night in the desert was extreme, and would be more so the further they marched.

The sound of a galloping horse broke the darkness causing Tagan and Sebastian to turn and face the noise. Out of the darkness emerged a group of riders lead by a very short person on a very small pony. The Field Marshal led his staff towards where Tagan and Sebastian sat upon their mounts.

"It is a grand sight would you not say my Princes?" Sylvester said as he drew closer, looking up at the two mounted figures," and I have the impression we are marching at a quicker pace so they can keep worm, I just hope we can keep this pace up!"

*****

Darkness had also fallen on Starlight and Dew as they huddled together for warmth. Neither had counted how many days had passed since they had lost Windfall, in fact neither of the fairies had spoken much, each deep in their own thoughts, words seemed too much effort and worthless.

"We must change direction again, we have been heading south for too long now." Starlight said in a low voice.

"Do you think they are still following us?" Dew asked.

"I don't know," Starlight said, "but what I do know is that if we don't complete our mission Windfall will have died for nothing, and I don't think I could live with that!"

"Alright we will change directions in the morning," Dew replied, "I would not like to think she died for nothing."

Hurriedly they gathered their few supplies and covered the signs of their nights camping, then without another word Dew took off and turned west again. Starlight watched her go then with wings spread out she ran as fast as she could, flapping her outstretched wings until she felt the steps she was taking became lighter and lighted, feeling she was airborne she gave some very hard flaps on her wings to gain height and pulled her legs up to reduce drag. Soon the barren desert floor was falling away below her as she sought a thermal, catching one she soared up into the dark blue early morning sky. When she judged she was at a desirable height she too turned west.

She scanned the desert far below her looking for Dew. After seeing a black dot moving quickly in a straight line she soon caught up sufficiently for her to make out Dew.

They flew like this for the rest of the day, Starlight occasionally dropping down to talk to Dew then gaining it again to look out for danger, which luckily she never saw. This routine continued for a few days, stopping only to eat and rest at midday when the sun was at its hottest. The journey seemed tedious, nothing changed, the stiffening hot sun, reflected by the featureless desert floor.

How many days they had been on this journey Starlight had lost count, it seemed like forever and she was beginning to doubt they would ever finish. Then she began to notice the build-up of cloud, not too much to begin with, just an odd fluffy white cloud in an otherwise clear blue sky. She took little notice of it but the next day there was more and even more the following day. She also saw what she thought was the very occasional speck of greenery. That evening when they stopped for the night she mentioned this to Dew.

"Yes, I have noticed more cloud, and in shady spots there is some thick type of grass growing, where the sun doesn't scorch it and kill it off. What do you think this means?"

"Rain, that is what it means," Starlight replied, "And if this area gets rain we must becoming close to the end of the desert!"

The next day they set off with a new enthusiasm, believing their journeys end was within sight. When Starlight saw a black line across the horizon below a dark cloud filled sky. By midday the features of high forest filled green mountains blocked their way. The excitement filled Starlight as she dropped down to Dew.

"I have never seen anything like this," Dew exclaimed as Starlight came into earshot, "It is a lot larger than the Dark Forest, you cannot see the edges!"

They stopped that night early in the shadow of the mountains, the temperature had dropped and developed into a pleasant evening.

"I think we should tackle the highlands tomorrow, it will not take us long to fly though them I would think, but then in one way the danger really begins." Starlight said as the lay on their bed rolls.

"What do you mean? I would have thought all our dangers were far behind us now, we have made it."

Starlight smiled, "Yes, we have made it, and the creatures are far behind us. But not everyone we will meet the other side of those mountains are friendly, in fact I would go as far as saying a lot are not, we just have to be on are guard as we head towards Kleve."

"Kleve? Why Kleve" Dew asked.

"That is where we will find Prince Tagan, and hopefully persuade him to send an army to help us." Starlight replied.

"What is Prince Tagan like, have you ever met him?"

"No, I have heard him speak and I have seen him many times, but I don't him," she replied.

*****

188

Tagan sat astride his mount watching the long column of his army marching into the darkness. It had been this way for a week now - marching all night and then just as the sun rose, before it gained its full heat, tents were pitched, meals eaten, horses fed and then sleep. The routine seemed monotonous and he had heard of mutterings from his troops. "But troops who were not moaning had lost all motivation," Lord Cogan had told him many years ago, so he did not feel disheartened.

Galloping horses distracted his thoughts, very soon he could make out the fingers of Prince Sebastian and Colonel Peabody in the darkness, accompanied by six other riders.

"Prince Tagan," Sebastian called as he drew close, "Colonel Peabody has bought some disturbing news from the Champion Lord, the Field Marshal and Lord Cogan is there already."

"Lead the way," Tagan replied and followed the others into the night. They crossed the march of the Champion Lord's army hand headed into the darkness of the desert, with no distinguishing land marks and a million flickering stars to light their way. Tagan was thinking they were lost when he noticed a light ahead, it looked like a burning torch.

As they rode closer to the light, Tagan could make out quite a large group made up of people, Trogs, the Guardian and Griffins, all milling around. A short distance away were standing a smaller group - it was to this smaller group they walked after they had dismounted.

Tim was the first of the group Tagan saw, then Lord Cogan, Sylvester, General Flintlock, of the Greater Longmans Army, who was providing an escort and last but not least Stickleback. It was Tim who spoke first.

"We have found a body. It appears to be that of a fairy!"

"A body! How did it get here, we only have two fairies with us don't we - Megan, your wife and Titus and I take it both of them are accounted for?" Tagan exclaimed.

"Yes they are both safe," Tim replied, "In fact it was one of Titus' patrols who found it just before dark. He said it was one of the clan fairies which makes it even more of a mystery as they can't fly!"

"But the clan fairies left Kleve in mass a long time ago - could it not be a casualty from then?" Prince Sebastian asked.

"Sorry for my crudeness, but no, the body is too fresh!" The unmistakable voice of Mortimer barked from out of the darkness. Then his face appeared in the torch light. "She has been dead for less than a week, but she met her death in a very violent way."

"So the fairy is a woman," Sylvester stated almost to himself, "and you have no idea how she died there or how she even got to be there?"

"No not at the moment, it will take me a lot more investigation to find out, and even then I may not have all the answers." Mortimer said. Sylvester looked at Mortimer for quite some time, as if summing up in his head all the facts, then said.

"Very well, do what you have to but don't be too long about it. I think this may hold some significance."

As he turned away, Mortimer said, "I cannot do my investigation on the back of a wagon, bumping along though the night, I must examine her body in daylight and that also goes for the area in which she was found."

Sylvester stopped in his tracks, and slowly turned around to face Mortimer.

"You do realise Mortimer that one of my concerns, and the reason I want answers quickly is that I'm beginning to think our enemies are closer than we think, and could strike at us any time." He said his gaze never dropping from Mortimer, his authority seemed to overwhelm his physical being, "I am unwilling to sacrifice any of my troops as an easy target, including you."

"I understand that," Mortimer replied, looking strangely a little bashful, "but Field Marshal if you want me to find the answers, the quickest way I can do that is by staying here and doing it tomorrow in daylight. I don't want to be away from the safety of the army for a moment longer than I have to."

"Very Well," Sylvester said, "Lord Champion, could you supply Mortimer with whatever he needs and an escort which can catch up with the army quickly when he has finished." Tim nodded in reply as Sylvester turned away, he heard him ordering the army forward again.

Tim looked at the small gathering remaining around him with Mortimer, Colonel Peabody and Major Gladstone in the middle.

"Colonel, I want you to provide an escort, small and able to move fast, but of a straight to be able to defend its self, and Mortimer."

"Yes my Lord, I will command it myself." Peabody replied, Tim gave him a questioning look, but said nothing. He did not like to get too involved in the running of each of his armies, leaving that to their commanders. Walking away he could hear orders being barked in the darkness, as they began to organise themselves.

*****

Peabody was glad to see the Champion Lord leave, he had no problems with him and found him a good boss who was willing to give his commanders their heads, but it was always nice to be left alone.

"Sir, I take it when you said you would command the escort yourself, you meant you would select the commander yourself?" Major Gladstone asked. Peabody looked at him, he was one of his two Majors, both of whom were good soldiers, but Gladstone was an ambitious person who was graced with boundless energy, he was properly volunteering for the command himself.

"No, Major, I meant what I said. Where is General Stickleback please?"

Soon an escort was arranged, comprised of Flying Wildbloods, camel mounted Scouts and three Griffins. Stickleback insisted on leaving a platoon of fifty Guardians. Looking at them Peabody was pleased - jointly they would not win a battle, but he was not thinking of a battle, they would however, be able to hold their own in a large skirmish, every one of them highly trained, and in most cases, tested combatant. Then Peabody saw a rider appearing on a horse from the shadows, he immediately know who it was, and felt a mixture of happiness and anger.

As Willow rode up to him he said in a harsh voice. "What are you doing here willow? You should be on your way with the army!"

"And I'm happy to see you as well," she answered calmly in her warm voice, which immediately disarmed any feeling of anger Peabody had at seeing her.

"You should have stayed with the army Willow, this is a dangerous situation to have put yourself in," he said as he helped her from her horse. Turning to him with a smile she replied.

"But I have confidence in you."

As the sun began to rise over the eastern horizon, a deep red on a cloudless morning it bought immediate heat, cutting through the bone chilling air. Mortimer set about his task with a speed which was astonishing for a man of his age. Peabody could see none of his troops, only the Griffins and their riders and two Guardians who were watching Mortimer intently.

"How long do you think it will take him?" Willow asked him from his side.

"I have no idea," he replied, "I suppose it depends on what he finds."

The sun raised quickly into the cloudless sky forcing up the temperature rapidly with every passing moment.

Chapter 17

"I don't think I have ever seen so much rain," Dew said as they huddled below a low branch of a large tree sheltering from the seemingly never ending downpour. She and Starlight had been stranded below the tree for two days now, as the constant rain fell. They had tried flying in it, but it battered Dew's wings threatening to damage them, and Starlight could not seem to break the cloud cover to bright sunlight which would help her to saw. Now they sat damp and disheartened wondering when the weather would break.

"We cannot just sit here, we must do something," Starlight said.

"I agree with you but what?" Dew replied.

Starlight looked at the unrelenting rain and the endless grey skies, they had come so far, to be stopped by the weather, and seemingly stranded.

"Walk" Starlight simply said, Dew looked at her, the question forming on her face, but before she could speak Starlight continued, "I have never seen rain like this in my life, and it seems to be too dangerous to fly, because we can't see enough. But before we regained the ability to fly again we had no option but to walk everywhere. So let's walk, we will get wet, but we would get wet anyway." With that, she dragged herself to her feet, picking up her few belongings.

"Well," Dew said, as she also got to her feet, "but how far will we have to walk?"

"That I'm afraid I cannot answer," Starlight replied, "The sky looks grey and overcast, but as rain falls from cloud we just have to walk to the edge of it, but where that is, is anyone's guess."

The two Fairies trudged through the pouring rain, with no escape from wetness. Each branch or leaf from the undergrowth was covered in water which dripped onto them as they pushed through. This on top of the rain which ran down their necks from their sodden hair, made the both of them feel miserable.

It was difficult to judge the time of day when they reached a small hamlet, but they could see the light of candles through the cracks in half open doors and shutters. The main street, if you could call the muddy lane with a few shacks lining each side a main street was deserted, not even a village dog could be seen cowering from the rain.

"I do not think a place this size would have an Inn, but let's see if there is somewhere warm where we can shelter out of this rain." Dew said, Starlight nodded her head, but said nothing in reply.

One house stood out from the rest by its size. It was over twice the size of all the other houses, which was not saying much, but the construction seemed of a more professional standard, and it had a second floor.

Walking up to a large, quite impressive front door, Starlight took a deep breath, looked at Dew for reassurance and then knocked. If they were hopping to hear an echo they were bitterly disappointed, the response seemed to be only silence. After what seemed like an age, standing in the dripping wet Dew said.

"Should we try knocking again, or going to another house?" Starlight knocked again, harder this time, although she thought she had knocked quite loudly the last time.

Suddenly the door swung quickly open inwards, and standing in the door way stood a very stocky, frightening looking woman. The wild black hair was sticking out in all directions, her chubby cheeks were divided by a thick set red nose, her eyes were deep set, but gave the impression of missing nothing as they darted between the two soaked fairies standing on her doorstep.

"WHAT?" she growled, in a thick country accent, her teeth seemed surprisingly white and bright between thick lips as she opened her mouth, which suddenly spread into a wide smile, giving her face which had looked angry and vicious, a warm, even motherly look. "I do believe we have fairies here. Bunt! Bunt! Come to the door and see who we have here." She shouted to someone unseen in the house. But before the unseen person who she was calling could respond she said to the two fairies, in a kindly almost hushed voice, which was a complete contrast to her ruff appearance.

"Come on in you poor darlings, you must be drenched." Hurrying the two fairies inside she never stopped talking, "This is Bunt, my love, don't be frightened of him he looks a brut of a man, but he is as gentle as a pussy cat really."

Indeed he certainly looked like his name, he looked a giant of a man overwhelming a small wooden chair on which he sat. Or the chair appeared to be small, but as Starlight sat on a chair close to the roaring fire she realised it was the same size as the one which Brut occupied.

His legs where spread out in front of him, large and thick, but not in a flabby way, his arms were also large, about the size of each of her legs. His board expanding chest sat upon a very wide stomach, which looked like rolls of fat as he sat, but his face was a contrast to the giant of a man. He looked kind, with rugged features which told a story of many years of weather-beaten work and wild dark hair culminating in a large bushy beard.

"Come sit you down here," he was saying in the quietest reassuring voice Starlight thought she had ever heard, and quite a contrast to the bull of a man. Dew sat on another chair near to the fire. "My Tina will get you some hot broth. You must be chilled to the bone!"

With that, Tina appeared with a large steaming bowl in each hand and gave each fairy one. Starlight could feel the warmth seeping through the cloth covering her hands, she was almost disappointed when Tina returned to give them each a spoon so Starlight had to let go with one hand.

Dew was already slurping her soup, and by the look of pleasure on her face was feeling the effect of the hat liquid on her body. Starlight spooned up a mouthful and drank it, the effect was immediate, she could feel the warm soup penetrating her cold body and heat radiating throughout. Another spoonful and another, and before she knew it she was scrapping the bottom of an empty bowl for more.

"Give it here girls. You look like you haven't eaten for a week," Tina said as she replaced the bowls with full ones, which were also soon dispatched. Burt looked on a small grin playing upon his lips as he watched the two fairies eating their fill. Then Tina hurried them into another small room where she gave them both large blankets and told them to remove their wet clothes.

When Starlight and Dew returned to the main room wrapped in their blankets, Brut didn't seem to have moved, but Tina was hurriedly hanging their wet clothing around the fire. As soon as she saw them, she said, "Come here a sit by the fire, I'm and then tell us how you came to be out on such an awful day?" They both sat down close to the fire, Starlight could feel the warmth seeping into her body, as if seeking her cold inner soul to give it life again. After settling herself, she looked at Dew who was doing the same. A moment of stillness passed as they looked at each other, without speaking they seemed to be each summing up the situation, and then Dew spoke.

"We are indeed Fairies, and we have travailed from the Dark Forest." Tina gasped, her mouth wide open, but Brut just snorted and nodded slowly.

"I had no idea that the Dark Forest really existed!" Tina exclaimed, "I thought it was only in stories to frighten naughty children."

"Oh, it exists alright," Brut said slowly, "but it is so far away across a barren inhospitable wilderness no one has ever travailed to or, up to now from it."

"You know about the Dark Forest?" Starlight asked.

"Only what I have been told by old wise men, they say it is an evil place full of dark magic and monsters, where Fairies plot to take over mankind and enslave us!"

"THAT IS ALL LIES!" Dew shouted, leaping to her feet and nearly dropping her blanket, only grabbing it at the last moment. Brut did not react, his eyes just slowly looked up at the fairy.

"That is something like the stories we were bought upon, and the reason, I am told why we had left the Dark

Forest in the first place." Starlight said slowly, each word delivered in a near hush. Dew looked at her, total shock written across her face.

"So, why did you all return to the Dark Forest if you think it is such an evil place?" Dew gasped, still unbelieving.

"Because there is greater evil in this world than just stories, and after Berberdoff and the other elders meet Princess Faith and some other of your fairies and saw how they helped Prince Tagan and the others who joined together to fight this evil, we thought we may have misjudged the Dark Forest, so when we received the call for all fairies to return we decided to go." Starlight explained.

"But in your hart of harts you still don't trust us," Dew said, "Why did you and Windfall join me on this journey?"

"But we do trust you, we trust you all," Starlight replied passionately, "We have had a long and hard struggle across the desert which took months to get to the Dark Forest first, remember we could not fly then, we had to walk, hundreds of our clan died from heat exhaustion and dehydration as a result. So we know what it is to cross the desert and that is why Willow and I joined you on this journey so we could get help - we know what it will take to return with an army!"

Silence filled the room as the two fairies were deep in their thoughts, only the snapping of burning wood in the fire broke the tension.

"They were only stories," Brut said eventually, "I will be honest but I never knew fairies really excited until now, no one as far as I know have ever seen one. So you two are quite a shock, I'd say."

"That is an important point which Brut has said." Tina said, "not meaning to be rude, but as you have both talked about evil in this world and never having seen a fairy before how do we know you even are fairies, you my dear haven't even got any wings?" The two fairies looked at each other, and then Starlight gathered the blanket to her front letting it fall from her back. She then unfolded her wings to their full extent, which nearly touched both walls of the room and very, very slowly flapped them causing a downdraft that made the fire roar. When she had finished, Dew did the same unfolding her wings, but she was able to take off and hover about a foot above the wooded floor boards, before settling back down and folding her wings again.

"That seems to settle any doubt about that," Brut said in a calm voice.

They talked into the night until the two fairies felt weariness taking over them, so Tina showed them to a stable which was connected to the house by a small door. The stable smelt of warmth and horses, one of which a large carthorse they were sharing. Settling into the warm dry straw they both slept the sleep of the just.

Waking the next day after the best night's sleep Starlight could remember she looked at Dew who was still sleeping. Lying back on the straw Starlight could hear the rain still hitting the roof. Later Tina appeared with some bread and milk which both fairies gratefully ate. Tina asked them to remain where they were as she did not wish to alarm any callers. She returned with more food for them at lunch time, and Brut opened the main stable door to take the horse out. They could then see the rain was still falling in sheets, with no glimmer of a break in the sky.

This routine continued for several days, Tina bringing them food and Brut taking the horse out for work, then returning it before night fall. The smell of the wet animal as Brut rubbed it down at the end of a hard day's work filled the stable with a warm reassuring smell. The evenings were spent in the main house by the roaring fire, but with every knock at the door they were soon shuffled back into hiding in the stable.

It was the fourth night when they had all settled by the fire to talk when Brut said, "I believe the rain will be clearing soon, it did not seem as intense today. Soon you two girls will be able to be on your way."

"Thank you, that will be...."

BANG! The front door flew in with the force of an explosion, being ripped off its hinges and landing across the floor. The four occupants leapt to their feet ready to face whatever danger together. Suddenly the room was full of hooded men holding clubs and chains.

Brut flew at the intruders in an instance, flooring two of the intruders with his massive clinched fists but the weight of numbers was soon too much as the clubs rained down on Burt's back and head. After what seemed like an eternity Brut still managed to lift his bloody face to his attackers with a pathetic pleading smile that never touched his burning eyes.

"BRUT NO!" Tina screamed as she launched forward.

"STOP!" a hooded man shouted. "I said stop!" he repeated until silence returned to the room apart from Tina's sobs as she cradled Burt's bloody and battered head.

"So the rumours are true, you are hiding monsters." The man said looking directly at the two fairies through holes cut in the hood. Starlight and Dew had not realised in the confusion that they had both stood with their wings unfolded for all to see. "Bring the monsters," the man commanded before turning and walking out. The two fairies were grabbed by strong ruff hands and bound with course rope before being bundled into the dark rainy night.

"I know your name Goodrith Melamear." Tina shouted into the night behind them as they left.

Starlight and Dew were half carried, half dragged down the muddy street, past all the houses and into the forest. No one spoke. The only noise was the snapping of twigs under foot and the drip, drip, drip of the rain falling through the tree canopy.

Soon the dark forest was illuminated by burning torches as they entered a large clearing under a very large oak tree. Here stood quite a number of people, a mixture of both men and women - their features hidden by the darkness only slight glimpses from the torch light revealed that none of these were wearing hoods.

Two stood out from the crowd, a tall thin man with wild grey hair, and a younger woman with long red hair. Here Starlight and Dew were stopped.

"What are these monsters which you bring before us?" The man asked in a deep hostile voice.

"They are witches!" the simple reply came. The red haired woman snorted then walked forward and around the two fairies, pulling at their wings as if to see if they were real or some sort of joke clothing, after she seemed content with what she was seeing she returned to standing beside the man.

"Whatever these two creatures are, they are certainly not witches. Witches can be for good or for evil, but one thing they cannot do is fly! I do not know if these creatures can in fact fly, but those wings are real and part of them."

"Why don't we find out if they can fly?" A shout came from the darkness in a gruff male voice.

"And let them escape if they can fly?!" the man shouted back, but his eyes never left the two fairies. "No, we must question them and find out the answers that way."

"If they truly are monsters, a few questions will not give us the answers, they may refuse to talk!" a woman asked from the line, but which one spoke it was hard to tell as they were all bathed in darkness.

"I do not intend to give them the opportunity not to answer," the man said, and then added, "take them to the blacksmiths'."

Hard hands grabbed their arms and forced them along as they left the cover of the trees the rain hit them again, not as intense but just as wet. They were marched out of the wood and to the edge of the village. Although they had not seen any of the village in daylight this part looked much more run down compared to the part where they had found shelter. They were pushed along by their four guards who kept a firm grip on their arms. Everyone else from the clearing seemed to have disappeared into the darkness, or more likely Starlight thought, back to their houses' to dry off and warm up.

Soon they were stood outside a larger building with a large stable type door, the man from the clearing, with the red haired woman alongside him, appeared from seemingly nowhere and the man rapped on the stable door with his fists making enough noises to wake the dead. After four or five more attempts at knocking the door a very angry, but muffled voice could be heard from the other side. Then the door partly opened and a shaft of light broke into the damp darkness, this was followed very quickly by a man's head, slightly bald but very angry. His eyes quickly glanced at the man and woman then took in the four hooded guards, but his longest looks were for the two fairies.

"You had better have a damn good reason for waking me up in the middle of the night, and why have you dragged those two young girls out of their beds on such an awful night by those four fools?"

"We have the most important reasons for waking you I assure you," the man replied, "and as for these two, they are not girls as you will soon find out."

Huffing in a most unconvincing way, he opened the door to let them enter. The inside was warm, to the far right in stables stood two horses that raised their heads to see who had disturbed their sleep but took no more notice. This was in sharp contrast to the woman who stumbled into the shed in her night clothes, covered with a very large shawl to keep her warm.

"Who was it dear, what did .....?" She stopped as her eyes fell onto the intruders.

"Who they are, my dear, is obvious," the blacksmith replied, "but as to what they want is not so clear yet?"

On seeing the two fairies the blacksmith's wife immediately said, "You poor girls look terrified and frozen, come with me and I will warm you up."

"NO, YOU WILL NOT TALK TO THE MONSTERS OR COMFORT THEM. Now please leave!" the man shouted.

"You," the blacksmith said in a very firm voice, "will mine your manors' when you speak to my wife. Now what have these two girls done to be treated in such a harsh way?"

"I am sorry." The man replied, "But we live through trying times. As to these two, it is here we intend to find out by questioning."

"Questing, how?"

"In such a way that they cannot help but give us answers we want!"

"You mean torturing them!" the blacksmith's wife said.

"That will not be necessary if they tell us what we want to know," the woman spoke for the first time.

"And what is it you want to know?" The blacksmith asked, his voice hardly covering the contempt he clearly felt.

"Who they are, where are they from and what do they want with us?"

The blacksmith walked over to the two fairies and stood a little way in front of them.

"I have no quarrel with you, after all I have not met you until now and do not wish to see you come to harm, why will you not just answers these few simple questions?"

"We could not give them any answers," Starlight said very quietly, her voice breaking with fear, "because we have not been asked any questions yet. We have nothing to hide." The blacksmith nodded, then said,

"They have asked some very general questions, maybe you could start with them?"

"Very well," Starlight said, "I am a clan fairy and my name is Starlight, my friend here is called Dew and she is a fairy from the Dark Forest, we are on a mission to Kleve to get help."

"Help, help for what?" The man demanded in a harsh voice, the blacksmith gave Starlight a slight reassuring smile and nod.

"The Dark Forest, where we come from has been surrounded by lizard like creatures whose intentions are unknown to us, but we do not believe them to be peaceful."

"You may be quite right. Those creatures seem to be similar to the creatures who have been ravishing the surrounding countryside," the blacksmith said looking at the man and woman.

"You say you're traveling to Kleve, but why should we believe you?" the woman said.

BANG! The barn door flew open startling all the occupants who looked in surprise to see a group of what looked like soldiers standing at the open entrance.

"I think we will take charge of these fairies," a deep strong voice, full of authority, said in the silence which had filled the barn. Starlight quickly flashed Dew a smile of reassurance - they had come to look for the army, and now they had found them!

"My Lord," the man began to reply, a little of the confidence seemed to have slipped from his voice, "we were merely trying to establish the motives of these two fairies."

"I think the Sheriff's Inquisitor will be able to find out everything which is needed, they are coming with us!" The commanding low voice, cut into the words of the man who bowed in respect. The four guards also backed away from the fairies as the soldiers drew close. The only person who did not move was the blacksmith. He had a cast down worried look on his face as he looked at the two fairies, then said in a low, hushed voice which was very hard for even Starlight to hear,

"I'm sorry."

Chapter 18

"Are you sure of the numbers which you saw?" Tagan asked again to the two female scouts, it was not that he did not believe them, but the amount of creatures which they were reporting took him quite by surprise.

"We are quite sure, Sire, we flew as close as we safely could," The slim Observer said in a confident tone. Quickly, it had been realised that using women as Observers were better than men due to their weight and ability "but they had flying creatures overhead so we could not over fly them." She continued.

"Were you seen?" Tagan asked.

"Most certainly," the other Observer replied, "but they did not seem to care that we were there or that we had seen them."

Tagan looked around the tent at the other senior commanders which were listening. Tim sat away from the map table at the back of the tent as if disinterested, but he would have heard the reports first before he bought the two Observers to the meeting. Lord Cogan stood rubbing his chin as he listened to the reports and intently studying the open maps on the table, beside him stood Prince Sebastian and

Stickleback. The only commander who did not seem to have an expression of deep concern, apart from Stickleback of course who never had an expression which anyone could read was Sylvester.

He was now looking at his fellow commanders, not at the map table or the Observers who had just finished conveying their message. He was the one who also broke the silence when they had finished speaking.

"Thank you very much for an excellent job," he said, "now I suggest you get back to your camp before nightfall stops your Griffins from flying." With the dismissal the two Observers left the tent with a slight nod to Tim who replied the nod with a smile.

"Well gentleman what do we think of that?" Sylvester asked. Tim now stood up and walked to the table to join the others in studying the map.

"They appear not to care about the fact that we saw them, five hundred are not a great deal in the size of an army, but also it is not a number which should simply be ignored!" Cogan said, and Tagan added,

"And who is to say these are the first group to have passed us, where are they heading and for what purpose?"

"Well I can answer both of those questions I believe," Tim cut in, "I can reassure you that no other groups have passed us, my scouts would have picked them up. I know our remit was to scout ahead of us to see if the way was clear, but we also carried out wide over the horizon patrols to the sides and rear, it makes good military sense," all the other commanders seemed to nod agreement in unison, "as to where they are heading, I can think of three possibilities, the most obvious is to disrupt our supply lines, second is to bypass us and attack our home lands again now that our army is out of the way and thirdly - to attack our group with Mortimer."

No one spoke as they all digested what Tim had said, Tagan thought just how much Tim had changed from the young lad he had first met to now being the Champion Lord. Sylvester broke into his thoughts,

"I think my Lord Champion you could be quite right, but if that is the case we have our supply lines as secure as we can get them with General Flintlock's army, as for them attacking our home lands, there is not much we can do about that at the moment, if ever."

"We will be able to sort them out when we get back!" Stickleback said.

Sylvester looked at him with sad eyes. "To be perfectly honest, General, I do not see us returning. We are greatly outnumbered, we have no secret weapon. I see it as our task to kill as many of the creatures as possible to reduce the numbers so when they do return to our homelands, which

I'm sure they will, the armies who meet them will outnumber them and be able to destroy them once and for all!"

"What armies?" Tagan asked.

"I have made contingency plans," Sylvester replied, "now to matters at hand if they stay on their present course they will miss Mortimer's party, but we cannot count on that. Lord Champion at first light I want a messenger to fly to Colonel Peabody and inform him of the danger, I will rely on him to make the judgment of the situation."

"Yes Sir," Tim replied then nodding towards Stickleback they both left the tent. As the tent flap was opened Tagan could hear the noise of the camp being dismantled for the nights march, further away from Mortimer and closer to the Destroyer's creatures.

"Do you really think this is a one way trip?" he asked quietly, Sylvester and Cogan stopped what they had been doing and looked at Tagan.

"I'm sorry Your Highness," Sylvester said in a low voice, "but I can see no other outcome, but we must do our duty whatever for those who we leave behind."

*****

Colonel Peabody watched the sun setting over the horizon to the west, the deep red globe casting long shadows across the featureless landscape. He knew just hidden out of sight scores of watchful eyes scanned outwards across the desert from numerous stand to positions. The soldiers would stay there until darkness surrounded the camp and then apart from the centres would silently return to their other duties which, after dark, mostly meant sleeping until their turn for guard duty. A camp at night, after it had been swallowed into darkness was as silent as a grave, no movement, no lights and very little whispered sound.

As Peabody stood and watched his camp disappear into the darkness, he quietly smiled to himself, he was proud of his well-disciplined professional army who had not even been formed a few months ago. He also felt confident they would perform well when called on to do so in battle, but this was dulled by a stab of pain for all those soldiers, both men and women who he would lose in the fight.

"You cannot see any one to command now, come into the tent and keep warm." The words made him jump with the suddenness of them, he had not heard Willow walk up behind him.

Looking at her he said, "Yes, you are right, I will come in now." Together, they walked the short distance to one of the only three tents which they had with them. One was a tent used by Mortimer to both undertake the post-mortem of the unknown Fairy, and to sleep. Another was for Willow and some of the other elder women who worked with her to live and sleep in, and the last one to which they headed was the command tent, which at this time of night doubled as a dining room for the few officers, the elder women and Mortimer.

As they opened the two tent flaps, very carefully and one at a time so as not to let any light out, they could hear low conversations and smell the warm food, this immediately made Peabody feel very hungry as he had not eaten since before sunrise. Inside the warm tent were three tables, one to the right separate from the other two, this was the operations table, covered in maps and reports, sitting behind this was one of the female flying scouts, this table was always staffed and it must have been her turn, Peabody racked his brain for her name, it did not matter but he took pride in knowing the names of all those who he commanded. Demby, yes that was it, he did not speak to her just nodded as she sat up on seeing him come into the tent.

The other two tables were set out for eating, several of the elder women and a few officers sat around one talking in low hushed voices, having finished their meals and the officers two male and one female were taking time to relax a little. On the other table all alone sat Mortimer slowly spooning his thick stew and dabbing in a crust of dry bread, he seemed to be lost in his thoughts.

"Do you mind if we join you," Willow asked him as they both sat down opposite him. Mortimer did not reply, but seemed surprised that anyone was there.

After they had both sat and been served with their large bowl of thick mutton stew and a crust of bread, Peabody asked, "I take it you have come up with some answers to the mystery of how this fairy got here and how she died?"

Mortimer looked at him with open mouth. "We buried her this afternoon, I don't think it would have been much use doing that if I still needed her body to find out any more answers!" Peabody looked at him with a stern look.

"I don't think you need to be sarcastic, I have not had the opportunity to speak to you since."

"Yes your right, and I apologise," Mortimer replied, "but I am tired and angry. Today we buried an unknown woman in the middle of nowhere, and for why?"

"That is what I'm asking you." Peabody said his voice a bit firmer now.

"I don't think we need to get heated, this has upset us all and everyone is feeling the strain." Willow said in a calm soothing voice.

Peabody and Mortimer nodded and then Mortimer said, "Right, I'm sorry to say I cannot tell you much more that what I thought a few days ago. She has been killed by something using a sharp cutting action, several times and maybe by more than one attacker. At a guess, I would say some of the flying creatures. Who she is and what she was doing is anyone's guess?"

"So," Peabody begins slowly to summarise what Mortimer had said, "We know she was a fairy?" Mortimer nodded, "We have no idea of her name, where she was going or why, we think she may have come from the Dark Forest, but we have no idea how she got here."

Mortimer was wagging his finger. "Yes to most of that," he said, "but I think I may know how she got here, she flew!"

"But I thought all along you had said her type of fairy could not fly?" Willow asked before Peabody could speak.

"And that is quite true," Mortimer replied, "the last time any of us came across this type of fairy they could not fly. But, during my examination I looked very carefully at the muscles which she used for her wings, and I would say she was well capable of flying!"

"In that case...." Peabody began.

"STAND TOO, STAND TOO!" Shouts rang through the silence of the camp, everyone in the tent immediately stopped talking to listen to the noise outside.

Then action, all at once the three officers ran out of the tent, Peabody leapt to the operations table just as a young runner entered the tent, looking at Peabody to one side and the duty person sitting behind the desk, he began shouting out his report to both. "We are under attack by an unknown numbers of creatures to the west, already elements of the attackers have broken though our boundaries!"

Turning towards the other remaining occupants of the tent who were all looking between surprised and worried Peabody said, in a very calm understanding voice, "Go and gather your belongings, there is a very strong possibility we may be moving very fast with little notice." This led to a scramble from the tent by the elder women, Willow and to a lesser degree Mortimer.

Following the quick evacuation of the tent, Peabody followed into the pitch dark night. The chill immediately caught his breath, then the shouting in the night as soldiers scrambled to their positions.

In a few minutes, all fell silent as soldiers steadied their breathing and tried to calm themselves before the attack began. Peabody stood alone in the darkness beside the tents, his ears and eyes straining to hear or see any movement in the darkness. The millions of stars twinkling in the cloudless sky, and the new moon just creeping over the Easton horizon, If this was an attack, Peabody thought, they could have not picked a more perfect night.

As time elapsed with nothing happening, Peabody was beginning to think it was a false alarm. He saw movement as different soldiers were directed to better positions, silently hurrying passed like ghosts, their features blurred in the darkness.

"AAAAAGH!!" The scream broke the silence of the night, followed by more and more as soldiers in the darkness engaged with the enemy. Further shouts and screams broke the night from different directions. This, Peabody thought, was not a skirmish from a lucky patrol.

"Sir, we have a large attack on the northern perimeter." A runner who appeared from out of the darkness snapped in a breathless sentence. "A force of about two hundred creatures has clashed with our Easton flank, but we are holding them." A voice from his back said, turning Peabody now saw a group of four or five runners all waiting to give their breathless reports. Peabody waited patiently for each report in turn before deciding what the best course of action was. It sounded like this was a major attack to the North, East and West. The obvious course of action would be to escape south, but this could be leading them into a trap, or at the very least sending them onto an unknown course.

Gathering more reports from runners which were now arriving and vanishing thick and fast, Peabody and a few officers and senior ranks who had also gathered began to understand a clearer pitcher of the situation, and to formulate the outline of a plan of action.

The South perimeter was not being attacked at all. From here, they were able to transfer a few soldiers to boost the defenders in other weaker places. The East was the next weakest attack, as if only to distract the defenders from other more pressing places, which were the East and especially the North. This was where the main attack seemed to be coming from.

Peabody's mined was racing as he read and reread the reports, at the same time other people were trying to make constructive suggestions. But all Peabody could think was that something did not seem right, but it just seemed to be beyond him at the moment to see it.

"Stop!" He held up his hand and the talking fell silent, to be replaced by the not so distant sounds of battle from the darkness. As he listened in the darkness a thought struck him like a bolt of lightning, in the darkness he could hear what all the reports could not tell him, why they were making no sense.

In a clear but quiet voice, he outlined his plan, which was received in complete silence, apart from the odd gasp of surprise from the darkness, but when asked if there were any questions, no one spoke. "Right," he said to Captain Summerbee, Scout leader, just as everyone else dispersed, "bring me the largest strongest Griffin you have and the smallest lightest flyer, and I don't need the air arrows."

"But Sir," she hesitated, but then carried on, "our Griffins only fly now with a flyer and two air arrows for defence, it is what we have been training hard for, and it works!"

"That Captain I have no doubt but this is a very special mission." With a quick nod and no more questions Captain Summerbee vanished into the darkness. The next person Peabody saw was Mortimer walking hurriedly over towards him, glancing over his shoulder at every little noise coming from the darkness. As he came close Peabody said.

"I'm glad it's you, Mortimer. I was about to send someone to find you."

"Well I'm here now, how can I help?" he asked, still moving his head side to side at every sound.

"I want to fly you out of here to the army on a Griffin."

"Fly me out?" Mortimer exclaimed. "I would be too heavy for a Griffin with its crew."

Peabody looked at Mortimer in the darkness, most of his features were hidden in shadow, but he looked a thin bony old man, what on Earth was he doing here?

"You are the only reason we are here now, your findings are important, so I would prefer it if you would leave to make our job fulfilled." Mortimer looked long at him before saying very low and slowly.

"I have most of my findings already written down in a report, it would take me little more than an hour to finish it and then that could be flown out."

"We may not have as much time as an hour," Peabody replied, "and beside that can a report answer all the questions which are bound to be asked?" Before Mortimer could say anything a very large shadow appeared, before they had time to react Captain Summerbee stepped into view accompanied by the smallest slimmest flyer Peabody had ever seen, he certainly thought he would have noticed such a young flyer.

"This is Peach and Manning, she is the smallest and lightest flyer and Manning is out strongest Griffin."

"How old are you Peach?" Peabody asked.

"I am fourteen summers Sir," the girl replied.

"She is one of our best flyers," Captain Summerbee replied to Peabody's unasked question.

"Very good," Peabody said, but then Mortimer suddenly leapt before he could continue. "What on Earth are you doing?" he exclaimed as he jumped away from the large shadow which emerged to be Manning, who had managed to silently move around behind him. "Were you sniffing me?!"

"You seem very familiar, very comforting, and very right," Manning replied in way of an explanation.

"Manning and Peach, I want you both to fly Mortimer out of here and to find the rest of the army. If you fly at night you will be hidden from danger in the darkness so you will not need your air arrows and the weight you save from that will be countered with Mortimer," Peabody said.

"What do we do when we get there?" Manning asked. Peabody gave him a questioning look and Manning continued, "Without out air arrows we cannot fly recognisance so we would be grounded. Mortimer looks so light I think I would be able to carry him and the air arrows with ease, and then we could still do the job we're here for!"

"Very well," Peabody replied, "I'll bow to your greater knowledge, but if in the unlikely event you fail to find the rest of the army, fly to the Dark Forest, it is too dangerous for you to be out here alone. Now get your rations and water, I want you in the air as soon as possible, then we can look at a way of getting ourselves out of this sickly situation."

With that Peach and Manning disappeared into the darkness with Mortimer a little way behind, Peabody silently wished them luck as Captain Summerbee followed after a quick salute. Finding himself alone the darkness seemed to envelop him, and the noise of fighting seemed louder and sharper. For a brief moment he felt scared!

A hand on his shoulder almost made him jump out of his skin, as he had not heard anyone approaching.

"Your plan is a good one, and although some people will die I believe you will save most of us." Willow said as she stepped in front of him, her smile and calmness reassured him and strengthened his resolve. With Willow by his side he quickly visited all his troops which were quite a mixture of men, women, Guardian and Griffins, a few words of reassurance to them to bust their spirits. The he received word that Mortimer had been flown out, now was the time to put his plan into action.

Everyone was gathered together into a defensive circle, all the carts had been left apart from a few to carry the wounded, Peabody had no intentions of leaving anyone who he could save, in the middle of the group where the wise women, the car drivers who's carts had been left behind and the walking wounded, between them the houses and camels all the rations and water had been distributed. The outer circle where the soldiers and Griffins, with the greater numbers at the front battling their way through the strongest force of creatures, the night was eliminated by sudden bursts of flame which the Griffins shot into the solid ranks of creatures to disperse them, a tactic which had not been thought of before and seemed to work very effectively.

This continued until they had broken the grip of the creatures, just before the sun broke on the eastern horizon the creatures had fled, but Peabody knew they would be back, and in greater numbers, he just hoped his small rag tag army would be able to survive whatever was thrown at them, he also hoped Mortimer had arrived safely to the army so as to not make this a waste of time.

As the sun raised and the heat grew, they carried on their way, stopping for water and rest regularly Peabody new they did not have the luxury to lie up during the day and only march at night. The creatures knew where they were and could attack them at any moment. To counter this two Griffins were sent up to look for the creatures so as to give warning of an attack.

This pattern continued throughout a very long hot tiring day. Just before dusk, to the east, the sight of winged animals was seen flying low over the horizon. Everyone braced for an attack until someone from the head of the Colum shouted, "They're Griffins!"

A surge of excitement quickly spread as the Griffins came clearly into sight, but what was more surprising was the amount of people riding them, each of the twenty or so Griffins had at least ten Guardians or Troggs on their backs. As soon as they landed the passengers alighted and joined the rag tag army, but flyers had also dismounted and were now gathering as many of the walking wounded and wise women as they could and began flying them out. This operation was repeated a further four times during the night and the following nights until most of the sick, wounded and wise women had been evacuated and replaced by fit fighting troops. The days were spent moving as quickly as they could, which became faster with trained fighting troops, Peabody felt his confidence rising along with everyone else's. This was a moment too soon - as the sun rose in the east on the morning of the fifth day following the attack it revealed a wall of creatures blocking their way.

"Our luck could not hold out forever," he said to no one in particular. This had come as somewhat of a surprise as he had kept the Griffins grounded during the day light hours so as not to give their position away to the creatures, this of course had the drawback of them not knowing where the creatures where. Well now they knew!

"Draw up into battle formation," Peabody ordered, then turning to Willow, "I wish you had gone with the rest when you had the opportunity, I cannot guarantee your safety."

"I have made my choice and I am happy with it," she smiled back.

The battle formation which they took up was that of a pointed wedge. The Guardian made up the point and sides, with their long shields making a solid wall. A couple of Griffins were also near the point of the wedge but hidden behind the shield wall until they were needed to shoot flame out at the creatures lines. Just behind them were mixtures of human, both male and female soldiers and Trogg infantry, and behind them mostly but not totally Trogg archers. This formation marched slowly but deliberately towards the wall of creatures.

As Peabody pushed his way forward to be near the point, the Guardian made way for him as they noticed who he was, he wanted to lead by example, but his mouth was dry and his stomach felt full of butterflies, this was not the first battle he had been in, nor would it be his last he thought, but he was a cavalry officer and not infantry and he felt venerable on foot. Gripping his sword firmly in his right hand he fell in pace just behind the front row.

THUD, THUD, THUD. The rhythm of the arrows hitting the shield wall began. Swish volley after volley of arrows headed out to rain a deadly down pore onto the enema. Yelps of pain rang out from the crowded soldiers behind him as the arrows found their mark, drowned out by the inhuman screams of pain as the Griffins poured fire into the massed ranks of creatures.

Then they met in a deadly game of pushing the others off the castle. Peabody thrust his sword between the shields in front every time he saw a small gap. He could not make out what he was thrusting at, but he knew some times he hit his mark, and they kept slowly marching on trampling anything which fell in front of them.

The heat grew to nearly boiling point as the sun rose in the clear morning sky, there seemed to be no air as they slowly but surely pressed forward. Sweat poured from every paw of his soaking skin, how long had this been going on? It seemed like forever, the same darkness and bodies beside, in front and behind of him.

"Come on, keep going," he heard a voice calling out urging on those around him, then he realised it was his horse voice coming from his dry mouth. He could hear shouting behind him but could not make out any words. Then a hand grabbed his shoulder, and before he could react a voice said in his ear.

"Sir, you really need to come and see this." Slipping out of the line, he made his way back through the tight ranks of the wedge, giving encouraging words to his soldiers as he went.

The breeze struck him as soon as he emerged from the tight ranks of the wedge into the looser rear. The sun was high, almost noon, he had not realized how many hours had passed, and he had to blink several times as his eyes adjusted to the bright sunshine.

"Sir you have to see this," he heard a voice say, then clearing his eyes he looked up and saw flying Wildbloods circling around overhead, occasionally one would shoot down below his horizon, then he saw cavalry, his own cavalry charging at the rear of the creatures, followed by infantry and Guardian's thousands of them. The Champion Lord was leading his army into battle against the creatures, which apart from the ones caught up in the fighting against his own forces seemed to be scattering. He then noticed other troops attacking from his rear, it took him a little time to recognise the uniforms of both the cavalry and infantry but then it came to him. The Greater Longmans Army.

The fighting went on for a few more hot and sticky hours, but Peabody knew now the outcome was decided and he had bought his small group of soldiers to safety, for the time being any way. Willow walked to him gleaming a smile, and for the first time, kissed him passionately. "I always knew you would keep us safe," she whispered in his ear.

"Colonel, you have done a fine job with little resources," the Lord Champion said as he dismounted.

"Thank you my Lord, but how come you have come back, I thought you all needed to push forward?" Peabody asked.

"We do, but we have located the main body of the creatures' army, and they are less than a day's march away. You have struck the first blow against them, well done."

Chapter 19

The routine of captivity was the same day after day. Starlight did not know how many days had passed since she and Dew had been taken prisoner or by whom or where they were being taken. Their arms were bound tightly behind their backs stopping them from unfolding their wings and flying off. They walked between two mounted guards who, although were not friendly, had stopped being spiteful and horrible to them.

She and Dew were allowed to talk to each other as they walked along, none of the guards had anything to say to them apart for the odd order. Then just after mid-afternoon a few hours before dark she thought the guards were told something which as the secret message was passed between them, seemed to make them very uneasy.

They stopped early for the night for a change, but Starlight thought the night camp seemed to have been chosen for defence, against who she could not think ten armed men would be too much for any bandits or robbers.

"What are you all worried about, you seem on edge?" Starlight asked as they were given their bowl of hot stew.

"Nothing that will affect you two," their guard replied before returning to sit a few yards away with his comrades, but still keeping a watchful eye on them.

"So you have noticed something wrong with them, I wonder what it could be?" Dew said quietly.

"I don't know and I cannot see if we could take advantage of it, or if it is putting us in more danger!" Starlight replied. They talked quietly to each other to pass the evening, as they always did. As the night drew in their guards became even tenser, if that was possible. But as the evening turned to night they relaxed a little, anything or anyone approaching the little camp would disturb the night animals which they could hear clearly in the forest.

Starlight and Dew slept under the blanket each had been given on the first night, it was taken off them each morning so they were unable to use them for warmth, or to ward off the rain which seemed to come every day.

They both slept well considering, but now they were well used to using the earth for a mattress and their arm as a pillow. They woke at first light to a symphony of bird song which filled the air and forest, a fire was still burning and they all started the day with a hot drink and some porridge. They could not complain about the food, in difference circumstances, like not being prisoners they would have felt quite well-treated.

They began their long journey again after the camp was quickly cleared up, but this time the guards seemed to take more care over hiding any evidence that they had spent the night. Looking back at the camp as they slowly walked away, Starlight had to remind herself that was in fact the place they had stayed such a good job was done.

If anything, their guards seemed even more jumpy today. The Officer barked out orders, but other than that no one spoke. Scouts seemed to be sent out a head in pairs, and other pairs would stay behind after they had left. Every single one of their guards seemed to be constantly surveying the forest as they passed though.

"I think they are expecting trouble!" Dew whispered to Starlight and she nodded in understanding, but apart from a sharp look from the officer, nothing was said.

As the sun was at its highest point in a clearing, they stopped, half the guards dismounted and filled water bags for the horses, Starlight and Dew took advantage and sat down. Several of the Guards, including the Officer looked at them for several moments but no one rebuked them. As the scouts returned to say all was clear ahead and no one was following them, the Mounted guards dismounted and four of the other ones mounted up and set off in pairs to check their surroundings.

It all happened so quickly and quietly Starlight did not realise anything was going on until Dew leapt to her feet staring towards the forest edge. Then Starlight following her gaze saw several armed men, some with swords and others with bows and arrows drew back as if to shoot at any moment. She slowly got to her feet so as not to draw attention to herself. She saw the officer and the guards slowly raise their hands out wide, she did the same and then noticed Dew had done likewise.

All the armed men were in the same uniform so Starlight thought they must be soldiers not bandits or robbers, but from which army she had no idea. But then no! She had seen that type of uniform or one very similar. Without a second thought she walked over to where the person who she took to being in charge was speaking to the officer. Dew after a moment's hesitation followed. Both men stopped talking as they approached - a questioning look on the newcomers face.

"Are you from the Mercian Army," she spurted out.

"Yes, we are," the man replied, "who are you?"

"We're prisoners of these people and we have a message for Prince Tagan," Starlight said in one breath.

The men looked back at her for a moment and then his glance fell onto Dew. No one moved. It was as if time stood still whilst he thought of a plan of action.

"Untie them," he spoke in a low gentle voice, but immediately two Mercian soldiers leapt forward to cut their binds. "You are a Fairy, and I take it so are you," he said looking at Dew, "what are you doing here and how did you get here?" he asked.

Rubbing her wrists Starlight said, "As I said we have a message for Prince Tagan. We have come from the Dark Forest and were sent by Royal Princess Faith to ask Prince Tagan for help, the Dark Forest has been surrounded by the Destroyers Creatures."

The Mercian Officer nodded and said, "I am Lieutenant Thursday, we will be happy to escort you safely to Kleve, but how did you become prisoners?" He looked at the officer.

"They were going to be lynched as witches by some towns folk, we decided it would be better to take them to the Inquisitor to see exactly what and who they were, and if they were dangerous," he replied.

"I can tell you what they are," Thursday said, "they are both Fairies. But what I want to know is how you got here, I know the Dark Forest is a very long way away over desert and you," he looked straight at Starlight. "Can't fly?"

"That has all changed since we got to the Dark Forest, now all Fairies can fly."

Lieutenant Thursday nodded then looked at the officer and his men who were being gathered together. "You have violated Mercia's severity with armed soldiers, we will escort you out of our country, but I must warn you Mercia is on a war footing at the moment, the next time you may well be interned."

"I am grateful," the Officer replied, "you will get no trouble from us."

Soon, Starlight and Dew found themselves on horseback holding on as their horses moved along quite quickly beneath them. Neither had ever ridden before, so they each hung onto the reins as they were led by another soldier on horseback. They had asked to be able to fly to Kleve but the Lieutenant had told them it would be safer if they stayed with him and his troops, they would be in Kleve in a few days.

The next few days seemed to fly past. All members of the troop, of which there was about one hundred, seemed very friendly and shared their food with the two fairies. They were given extra blankets to keep warm on the cold nights. At night to the light of the camp fires they told the soldiers of the Dark Forest, and they told Dew about Kleve and Queen Kathryn and Starlight about what had changed since the Clan Fairies had left, she even got to meet some soldiers who remembered her the last time she had been in Kleve.

But it was with a feeling of relief when Starlight looked down at the walled city of Kleve, with the river meandering around and the towers of the palace standing out in the mid-morning sunlight.

They entered the city walls and as a group made their way straight to the palace. In the palace courtyard they dismounted and then Lieutenant Thursday showed them inside, through the ornate corridors towards the throne room. Standing outside the two great doors Starlight looked at Dew, Dew gave her a slight smile which never touched her worried looking eyes. Starlight smiled back in encouragement but she felt sick to her stomach with worry.

The doors opened to reveal a bright room, with gold and white columns and gold framed mirrors reflecting the light of hundreds of candles and the sun light pouring through the windows. At the far end stood on two plinths two thrones, one very large and ornate with gold, purple and red shining stones reflecting the light, the second throne was slightly lower smaller and less ornate, but still impressive. Guards stood at regular intervals down each of the two long walls, each adorned with shining breast plates and helmets.

All the Guards seemed to brace up at the same time without an audible order, and then the Queen appeared and quickly walked to the larger throne and sat down. Lieutenant Thursday bowed down and Starlight and Dew followed suit.

After a slight signal, almost undetectable, from the Queen, Lieutenant Thursday said, "Your Majesty, these are two Fairies from the Dark Forest with a message for Prince Tagan."

"Indeed, well please step forward and tell me about yourselves," the Queen said.

Both Fairies took a small step forward and gave a slight bow of their heads, then Dew said, "Your Majesty, we have been sent from Royal Princess Faith with a request of help from Prince Tagan as the Dark Forest has been surrounded by the Destroyers Creatures."

The Queen nodded as she listened, looking intently at the two Fairies. "I have some good news and some bad news for you," the Queen replied. "We already know about the creatures and about the Dark Forest and as we speak we have three armies heading towards there. I am surprised you did not bump into them on your way here. But I have two questions for you, first - how is Faith and second - how did you get here, as far as I know only one of you can fly?"

The Fairies took a quick look at each other, and then Starlight spoke, "Your Majesty, Royal Princess Faith was very well when we left. I know when we were last here we could not fly, but since we have returned to the Dark Forest we have had the ability to fly return to us. We are glad that some armies have already left to go to the Dark Forest, but we had to make a detour to the south as we were attacked by some flying creatures, there was another one of us but she has gone missing since that day. We don't know what has become of her."

The Queen nodded as she listened, but before she could reply Dew said, "Your Majesty could I ask if you have seen Princess Megan, is she safe and well?"

The Queen smiled at this question. "Ah Megan, yes she was well last time I saw her, but as to her safety at the moment I could not say, she has gone with her husband the Champion Lord who leads one of the armies." Dew looked shocked at this news, but said in a calm voice.

"Thank you, Your Majesty, but who is Lord Champion?"

The Queen smiled in reply. "He came with her from the Dark Forest but when he arrived at Kleve he had an army made up of Guardian, Griffins and humans, his name was Tim, Faith knows him."

Dew nodded as her face showed a little recognition at the name 'Tim'. The Queen then stood. "I believe you must be tired after such a long journey. You will be shown to your rooms where you can rest and freshen up, and we will speak later in a less formal setting." Then she walked out and a servant appeared to show them to their rooms.

Turning to Lieutenant Thursday, Starlight said, "Thank you for all you have done."

"It has been my pleasure," he replied, "if you need showing around later, just give me a call."

The Fairies then followed the servant out of another door which leads to another corridor, which was lower but just as ornate. After a few turns he stopped outside a door and opened it in and indicated for Dew to enter, then he did the same for Starlight at the next door.

Entering the room, Starlight looked around in amazement. She had stayed in the palace but not in so grand a room. Seeing the bed tiredness overcame her, she jumped on top of the soft bed without getting into it and as soon as her head lay on the pillow she was in a deep sleep.

*****

Faith stood on the watch tower, high on the edge of the Dark Forest overlooking the vast dessert the sun backing all below it. Thousands upon thousands of dark figures milling around, as the creatures went about their daily routine, seemingly unaware of the three vast armies now appearing on the horizon.

"I think we will have a grandstand view of a great and glorious battle," Chancellor Becket said from just behind her, standing beside him was Berberdoff who did not speak.

"I have only seen one battle in my life," Faith said, "and I would never use the word glorious to describe it, it was horrid." Chancellor Becket gave her a sideway look, and then looked out again towards the far horizon.

"What I would like to know," he continued, "is why are they here, what right have they got for coming all this way to fight one of their battles, the creatures although large in numbers were doing nothing to harm us, and we did not ask them to interfere?!"

"I did," said Faith almost under her breath, then with a little more force, "I sent messengers to Prince Tagan to ask him to bring an army here to fight the creatures, I have seen first-hand what they are capable of and do not want the Dark Forest to fall under that terrene."

"When?" Becket gasped, the shock written plainly all over his face.

"It must have been months ago now," Berberdoff said almost to himself.

Becket looked daggers at him. "You knew as well, when was someone going to have the curtesy to inform me? Does the King know?"

Faith turned away from looking out towards the two men. She looked calm and collected, she had known one day he would be asking these questions, and most likely think a conspiracy had been going on behind his back, which in one way it had. "No the King does not know, he is in too a frail state to be bothered with these matters. The reason we did not inform you was because you had enough on your plate with matters of state, and as the Princess Royal I believe I had the authority to enact such a plan."

"Well Royal Princess, I do not know if you do have the authority to take such action, you are not the head of state yet and I take it you have not consulted the Council or I would have heard about it, and I would have objected strongly, as I'm sure your father and the Council would have. Do you realise what dangers you may have unleashed on all of us now?" Chancellor Becket said in a strong firm voice, which hardly concealed his anger. But before Faith could reply he turned around and quickly made his way off the viewing platform.

"I think you have hurt his pride," Berberdoff said to Faith as Becket left, "but I think once he realises the situation we are in Royal Princess, he will come to realise the action which you have taken was the right one."

"I hope you're right," Faith replied, "the only thing that concerns me now is why Dew, Starlight and Windfall didn't give us warning the armies were arriving and how was Prince Tagan able to organise and move such a large army in such a short time. I was not expecting him to turn up for several months yet."

"He is here now and with not one but three armies. Let us be grateful for small murices," Berberdoff said.

They both stood on the viewing platform looking across to the armies on the horizon growing larger in both size and detail, but after doing this for several hours alone, Berberdoff having left silently some time before, it began to occur to her. Now the three armies were in clear view, details of soldiers, archers and cavalry could be made out. They would still be heavily outnumbered by the Destroyers Creatures, who still seemed to be taking no notice of the new arrivals. She hoped that just over the horizon where more armies still moving towards them and she could only see the spearhead.

Chapter 20

Tagan was beginning to have similar thoughts about numbers as he stood up on his stirrups to gain the best view possible. Prince Sebastian was doing the same thing on his mount as were several of Tagan's Commanders, Major General Windfill, Commandant Stockton and Marine General Butterworth among them. Just behind the mounted men stood Field Marshal Roderick Sylvester Hungerford on top of a cart with a viewing glass to his eye in order to afford a better view. Stood beside him, shielding his eyes from the glaring sun, was General Lord Cogan.

"Good military doctoring states to gain a good victory you should aim to outnumber your enemy by about three to one," Sylvester said out loud to no one in particular, but everyone in general, "but it seems we are outnumbered by far greater numbers than that!"

"We cannot just turn around and go back," Lord Cogan said, probably without thinking.

Sylvester jumped down from the card huffing heavily, and then looking up at Cogan said, "I have no intention of turning around and before you ask I have no intentions of losing. We have come here to destroy these creatures once and for all and that is exactly what I intend to do. But right now I do not know how?" Tagan turned to look at Sylvester as he added, "I want everyone to go away for an hour and think on this problem, I think I will need all the advice I can take."

With that, the small group split up. Tagan remained sitting looking at the massed huddle of creatures.

"Do you have any thoughts to help the Field Marshal?" Prince Sebastian asked Tagan from his side.

Tagan looked at him as if he had forgotten he was there. "No, sorry I haven't, the only way I can see is if we thin out their ranks but the result of that would be we would all be killed before they are. This is quite a problem?"

About an hour later, the same group of officers where gathered in the cooler shade of the main command tent of Sylvester's headquarters, their numbers had been increased by Tim, Stickleback and Colonel Peabody looking very dusty and tired, a good wash and sleep looked more of what he needed than a briefing of idea's. Noticeable by her absence was Megan, who never seemed to be far from Tim, but the centre of attention as he liked to be was Mortimer he was giving his audience a report of his findings, he would have to repeat them when Sylvester arrived but this did not seem to put him off. Tagan listened intently.

"The body was that of a female Fairy of the Clan dependency, I believe from my examination she was quite young, fit and well fed, and the most amazing discovery I found is that she could fly!"

The tent door flap opened allowing Sylvester, Lord Cogan and their staff officers in. The tent fell silent. The only noise was the expectant shuffling of feet as everyone attempted to get a good position around the large map table.

Slowly looking around the tent at the gathered officers, Sylvester's eyes fell on Tim and Peabody. "Thank you for joining us Lord Champion, and a very warm welcome to you Colonel you and your troops are a fine example to us all, I am very proud of you and I'm sure the Lord Champion feels the same." Then looking at Mortimer he said, "I know you have been telling the other officers of your finding Mortimer and will I be very interested to hear a full report from you, but at the moment we have a more pressing problem."

"Should I leave?" Mortimer asked.

"No, I always welcome your input and you may have discovered knowledge which is useful for us, and I am glad to see you back safe and well."

Before Mortimer could reply, Sylvester bought the meeting to a start with asking for any ideas. He listened intently to the thoughts of some of the greatest military minds gathered together, never interrupting them, but asking a few questions to aid understanding, other officers also asked questions when it was not their turn to give their opinion. Sylvester noted down points on a pad of paper which grew larger with every opinion. After a few hours the meeting broke up with Sylvester thanking everyone and telling them he would call another briefing later when he had read all the advice and devised a plan.

Tagan walked out of the tent and the late afternoon hit him causing him to sweat immediately.

"What chance do you really think we have?" Tim asked from his side.

Tagan had not heard him walk up to him. "I do not know, but as long as we are here we must have some chance of winning, I am just not too sure of how many of us will still be around to see it," Tagan replied almost in a whisper.

*****

The tap on the door was quickly followed by its opening and a footman announcing in a load clear voice, "Her Majesty Queen Kathryn of Mercia," the Queen swept into the apartment as Dew and Starlight jumped to their feet. This was the first time they had hears anything from the Queen since they had arrived in Kleve a week ago and they were beginning to think they were an embarrassment that was best forgotten about.

The Queen was looking as regale as the last time they had seen her in the throne but this time her manor seemed to ooze authority, following a short distance behind her was a much smaller older looking man, with a fixed brow and a worried look on his face, he slightly smiled when he saw the two fairies but it only stayed on his lips.

"Please, please sit down. I have only come to see how you are and how we have been keeping our guests," the Queen said as she took a vacant seat, and then waving a hand at the gentleman added, "This is Lord Avon, he is the Commander of the Army of Mercia, I thought you may have some questions which he could answer." Lord Avon sat in another empty chair. Starlight and Dew exchanged a quick look with each other then sat back on the large settee which they had been occupying.

"The question I think we both have, Your Majesty, is have we done something wrong? We have been here a week and no one has spoken to us, we are not complaining about how we have been looked after. But it is as if we are being ignored!" Dew said as Starlight nodded with every word said.

Before the Queen could answer, Lord Avon said, "You're Majesty, if I may?" After receiving the Queen's nod, he continued, "I am sorry if you feel we have been ignoring you, but let me assure you we have not. I am here to tell you what we have been doing and the latest information." Both fairies sat back to take in all the information.

"We have sent off three armies under the command of Field Marshal Roderick Sylvester Hungerford a Trog, who I believe to be a more than capable leader, Prince Tagan, who your message was for is commanding one of those armies. Today in fact I have received the news that they have arrived on the outside of the Dark Forest and are within striking distance of the creatures, which I am to understand will be within the next few days!" Avon looked at the two fairies as he spoke, his face was calm but strained.

"I also believe you mentioned to the Queen that when you set off there were three of you?"

"That's right, her name was Windfall, she was like me, but we lost her when we were attacked by the flying creatures, we turned south and hoped she would follow, but we never saw her again," Starlight said quietly.

"Well," Lord Avon said in reply, "I don't know if this will be of comfort to you but we have found Windfall's body and she has now been buried."

"Thank you," Dew replied as tears rolled down Starlight's face. The news was not unexpected Starlight thought, but to hear it was still a shock. She had known Windfall all her life she was her best friend, in fact more like a sister. Lord Avon readjusted his sitting position, he seemed uncountable seeing the two fairies so upset, but it was the Queen who spoke.

"After this is all over, she will be honoured along with all the other heroes who gave their lives for the course of ridding the world of the creatures, I can assure you Windfall will not be forgotten by the people of Mercia."

"Thank you," Starlight said as she wiped her eyes, "I know she will not be forgotten, but now I think is the time for action. I think if you agree, Dew, we must be making our way back to the Dark Forest and tell the Royal Princess that we did succeed in delivering her message, even if it was a bit late."

"I think you completed you task very well, we now know that our actions are supported by the Dark Forest fairies and we are not wasting time and lives trying to help them. I will get a message up to the Field Marshal today. I think that will strengthen the resolve of all the armies," Avon said. "When will you be leaving?"

"As soon as we can," Dew replied, "we must get back and tell the Royal Princess the news as quickly as possible!"

"Well, not before tomorrow," the Queen said, "today you must get rest and provisions, and Lord Avon will send word that you are going. Lord Avon will also instruct you how to follow the route. We have Griffins flying it every day so you will be in good company, safer and not get lost." With that, she stood up to leave, followed by Lord Avon and the two fairies, they all thanked the Queen for all she had done.

"Poor Windfall, I hope she didn't suffer," Dew said in the silence which filled the room as the two fairies sat alone.

"Right!" Starlight said as she jumped to her feet, "we still have a mission to complete, there is a war going on and I do not intend to sit here in safety when so many will die, as Windfall already has. Let's get ready for our return journey so we can set out at first light in the morning."

*****

"Where is Chancellor Becket? He seems to have been very aloof and getting even later for these meeting since the armies have arrived!" Berberdoff repeated for the third time within a few minutes as he paced up and down the room wearing a hole in the thick carpet. The large room was silent apart from the noise of Berberdoff's shoes on the carpet and the occasional clearing of his throat which was beginning to annoy Faith!

This was one of the daily meetings so the three most important people in the Dark Forest could tell each other about what was happening, so nothing came as a surprise, once a week Faith chaired the council, but this was more informal and in her opinion more productive. It was one of the measures she had put into place when it appeared there would be a very large battle just outside the Dark Forest, and no one could predict how it would affect them.

The first hint of something wrong was the heavy thud of running boots in the corridor, and then the heavy door bursting open to reveal a very scruffy, unshaven and sweaty looking Chancellor, he had the look of fear written into every line of his wrinkled face.

"IT'S DEATH! I THINK HE'S DEAD!" he gasped between breaths.

Faith and Berberdoff exchanged surprised looks with each other and then Berberdoff said, "Of course, Death's dead that is the whole point of him!"

"No, no you don't understand," Becket said from his position near to the door where he was bent over double, holding on to the door frame trying to recover his breath, "He is hanging up by chains in one of the dungeons!"

"Dungeons! What do you mean dungeons?" Faith exclaimed in a shocked voice, she had never heard of anything like a dungeon in the Dark Forest, why would they need them, why would they ever have needed them?

"What were you doing in the dungeons to have seen this?" Berberdoff asked in a much more reasoned voice. They both stood watching Becket as he slowly made his way to a chair near to where they were and sat down. Faith and Berberdoff sat in seats close-by.

"The Dark Forest has always had dungeons Royal Princess," Chancellor Becket said between deep breaths, "they were created by magic in a dark time a very long time ago when the world was a very different place. Now they are almost derelict no one goes down to them. They are full of water and the in many places the roof has fallen in."

"I ask again, what were you doing there?" Berberdoff said. Becket gave him a long look before answering.

"I had heard that there was a tunnel leading from them out into the desert far from the bounds of the Dark Forest, I thought it could be a good escape route if the worst comes to the worst."

"Very good," Faith said, and then added, "did you find it?" Becket sat back, he seemed to have now recovered.

"No, I'm sorry Royal Princess I did not, I came back as quickly as I could when I had seen what I found, but I will return and fined the answer."

"No," Berberdoff said, "you have enough on your plate, and Chancellor you are not a young man any more, you should not be scrambling through dark wet tunnels at your age, no I will go and look, and I'll see what state Death is in."

Becket nodded slowly, "Thank you," he said.

"Well," Faith said jumping to her feet, "I'll accompany you. I'm younger than both of you and I have no duties which will be missed."

Berberdoff looked surprised at Faith's reaction. "Well, Royal Princess, I would be honoured by your joining me," he said carefully, "if you are do you not think it may be prudent for us to take an armed escort, after all we do not know how Death got into the state which the Chancellor has reported, and if the tunnels are an escape route, the creatures could also find the other entrance and use it as a route in. We should be prepared."

"Very good," Faith said, she could see the logic in Berberdoff's points, but she did want to do something! "Please make all the arrangements as quickly as possible."

With that, the two men took their que and left. Faith sat and looked at the empty room, she had a feeling of both excitement and dread. Excitement of discovery of the tunnels and where they may lead, but dread in the news of Death. Who or what could have the power or inclination to hang up Death as if he was dead?

* * * * *

Tim helped Megan dismount from behind him, she still preferred to ride behind him the few times she did ride a horse, he thought and hoped it was just an excuse for her to be near him. Then he dismounted himself handing the reins to a close-by soldier, they were joined almost immediately by Colonel Peabody, Major Gladstone, Major Lord Bazzington and last but certainly not lest Stickleback, together all six of them walked towards the very large tent of the Command post. As they drew near to the entrance they joined a queue of other officers and commanders of the armies.

Inside was dark and noisy with the chatter of the occupants, the only light came from a single latten hanging from the tents roof over a quite large map table in the centre of the tent. There were chairs for the senior commanders to sit around the table and Tim, Megan and Stickleback took them with the other three and their staff standing behind them. Looking around the tent, Tim nodded to Tagan and Prince Sebastian. He noticed Marine General Butterworth, General Sidney Goberton, Commandant Stockton and Mortimer McMullan, sitting on a chair but casting very disdainful looks at everyone surrounding him. As his glance fell on Tim, Tim smiled warmly and a slight shadow of a smile in acknowledgement flickered briefly across his face.

"ROOM, ROOM SHUN!" was ordered by an old distinguished-looking Trog soldier and the tent quickly fell silent. General Lord Cogan entered followed by the Sylvester, he slowly looked around the crowded tent, then accompanied by complete silence made his way to a small platform, which he mounted. Despite being almost the smallest person in the tent, he seemed to fill it with authority, he was the Commander and everybody knew and respected him. Lord Cogan went and stood beside Sylvester, despite the fact Sylvester was standing on a platform Cogan still towered over him, but it was Sylvester who commanded the attention of the occupants of the tent.

"Thank you, Lady and Gentlemen," Sylvester said breaking the silence, the first point of business I would like to address is towards Mortimer and Colonel Peabody. I wish to say thank you for all your efforts regarding the body of the dead fairy, and Colonel I hope you will pass on my thanks to all your soldiers, they all played a very professional role and gave the creatures something to think about."

Peabody nodded and smiled, silently mouthing the words "I will". Then Sylvester continued. "Mortimer, thank you for your report which I have read with great inters, and I can now tell you your conclusions were right. She was a fairy named Windfall, I have received a message from Kleve confirming this and also telling me she was one of three taking a message from the Royal Princess Faith asking for help. The other two fairies were able to complete their mission, and yes Mortimer she could fly." The tent was filled with a murmur as the information was digested.

"Now we come to the reason we are here." Sylvester explained his plan and everyone's part in it. The three armies would not attack the enemy in one block but at several points at once - quite far apart. This way they could penetrate the enemy ranks at points of their choosing and locally outnumber them. The cavalry would harass the edges picking off any creatures that became dislodged from the main group. Sylvester spelt out their slim chances of success but there was a chance they could make it happen and, he pointed out, if he did not believe they would win he would never have accepted the commission in the first place.

After the outline of the plan, Sylvester and Cogan covered every bit of the plan, including all concerned people, in detail. Several hours later, when the briefing was over, no-one in the tent was in any doubt what their job was and what was expected of them. Now they had a night to relay that to their soldier - the battle would begin at first light.

Chapter 21

The early morning chill still hung in the air and every word spoken was accompanied by the warm moisture of breath. A hundred different smells filled the air from hundreds of small fires all cooking an eagerly awaited hot meal to warm the bones of thousands of chilly soldiers. Looking up, Tim could see a million stars in the still dark night. Very soon, the first glimpses of dawn would creep above the eastern horizon.

"Today is the day we have been planning and looking forward to for months," he heard Megan say behind him, he turned around to see her beautiful but worried face, "I'm frightened - be safe, I could not live if I lost you my beloved."

"Don't worry about me," Tim replied with a reassuring smile, which he did not feel himself, "you make sure you look after yourself, and don't take any risks." He then took her in his arms and they kissed passionately, lingering for as long as they could to feel the comfort in each other's presence.

"My Lord Champion, the Wildbloods await," a Guardian messenger said in a low voice. Kissing Megan one last time, Tim turned and followed the soldier.

The Guardian army was lined up in four great columns with the Wildbloods making up the second column, between them stood dismounted cavalry doing their last minute adjustments to the mounts. Tim was surprised though to see several Griffins with their flight crews, but he remembered the suggestion which Colonel Peabody had made, it would be interesting to see how that worked.

Tim would be the only army commander to be in the thick of the battle from the very start, his job was to lead by example, which meant to be on the front row of the Wildbloods attack, it was the Guardians way, which he was quite happy about, Tim had no illusions about his military and tactical knowledge, he was no Tagan, Cogan or Stickleback, he had not spent a life learning about battles and how to win them, he, as he admitted to himself was the son of a woods man who had stumbled into this life, but he was brave and could swing a sword with the best of them, if the Guardian wanted to follow a man who would push forward despite the odds, Tim was that man.

"My Lord Champion," Stickleback said as he saw Tim approach, "I believe we are as ready as we can be, every man, woman, Trog, griffin and horse has been fed and watered and they all know their position and responsibilities, as soon as we get the word we will be ready."

"Thank you, Stickleback," Tim replied, then looking up at the waning sky with the light of the Easton horizon becoming brighter, "I do not think it will be too long now.

259

Wishing the time to fly past for the start of a battle seems so stupid, but that is what I'm doing."

"That is not unnatural," Stickleback said, "it is coming and there is nothing we can do to avoid it, so we might as well get on with it. The waiting is always the hard part."

*****

In the command tent, Sylvester was thinking the same. He stood beside the great map table looking at the positions of all his forces and the thought position of the creatures. He had not been able to sleep, so he had stood over the map table, going through his plans again and again. It was a good plan, but he knew it was not a winning plan, not with the size of the forces he had. Should they just turn round and go back again? Was the thought going around and round his head, was he condemning his armies to certain death for nothing, the creatures would still be there, and maybe stronger! He had made plans, secret plans for other armies to fight what remained of the creatures when they returned to the wetlands. But none of the countries and kingdoms had been willing to supply troops or say openly they would commit to this. He only hoped they would keep their secret word.

"The sun is rising," a staff officer said poking his head through a gap in the tent door. Sylvester nodded but did not reply or look to see who the officer was, it would start soon and all the best made plans would collapse, he would then have to react and anticipate, hoping his decisions would not cost his troops lives wastefully.

Picking up his hat, he walked outside. Already the heat of the sun could be felt as long dawn shadows stretched out from every object. Looking around his was a hive of activity, with soldiers of all types making their final preparations.

"It will be a clear day for the slaughter." Mortimer said in a dry voice, Sylvester who had not heard him approach looked up at him. Mortimer had set up the field hospital for the sick and wounded, how many it would help anyone could guess, but every soldier needed hope of survival if they were wounded.

"I hope it is not going to be a slaughter, not of our troops anyway," Sylvester replied.

"I'm sorry but it is the only way I can describe a battle," Mortimer said almost to himself.

"If you can think of another way of dealing with this situation, even at this late hour, I would be grateful to hear?" Sylvester replied.

"No, I have no great ideas," he replied glumly. Both stood in silence watching the sun rise.

The dark red eastern sky made Sylvester think of blood, which he really would have preferred not to, then to his relief Mortimer said, "I will be off to the Aid Post. We are ready but last minute checks will not go amiss." With that he silently departed, much in the same manner in which he had arrived.

Sylvester looked again at the rising sun. It would be very soon that he would give the order for the battle to begin. Then it would be down to courage, training and the greatest luck he could hope for, most commanders would say it was their plans, but Sylvester was a realist, luck would play its part this day, for good or for bad!

"Good Luck Sylvester," Tagan called out to him as he rode passed with Prince Sebastian riding beside him, Tagan looked full of confidence, but Sylvester thought he would not expect anything more from him, he was a hardened battle commander and his feelings would be felt by his troops. Prince Sebastian, on the other hand, looked pale with a forced smile. He looked like he had not slept all night.

"Sir, the sun has risen above the forest and your orders are anticipated?" a young Trog Officer said a few foot behind him. Sylvester looked towards the Dart Forest and could see the sun just visible above the top of the canopy.

"Very good," he said turning to the Officer, "Unleash hell!" Hurrying away the Officer relayed the order. Sylvester was intending to follow the battle from his Command tent, but he lingered for a moment and looked back at his army. All was still and unnervingly quiet. He drank in the peace and calm.

WOOSH! Suddenly, the sky was blackened by thousands of arrows heading on their deadly course, the battle had begun!

*****

"Ready, draw, loose," Tagan repeated again and again in a calm but load voice, setting a steady rhythm for his archers. He was now walking along the rows of archers encouraging them, along with all the other thousands of archers from the other armies they were required to keep this up at a steady pace for an hour, armorers, who had been solidly making arrows for this very moment for the last month, carried arrows by the arm full between the rows of archers, sticking them head first into the ground near to their drawing hand so they would not fall behind the rhythm.

The idea Sylvester had said was to wear down the enemy before the armies drew near to each other, but very soon, as Sylvester had predicted, deadly arrows begin falling on their own troops, not to the scale, but still enough to distract anyone who was hit and those around them.

"Steady, hold your positions," Tagan said as he walked the ranks. The incoming arrows were a distraction, but he held onto the fact that there were not many in comparison and the hope the outgoing arrows were hitting their mark.

"Prince Tagan, the army is about to advance," a mounted runner reported.

Nodding an acknowledgement, Tagan hurried to his horse and pulled himself up onto the saddle, turning to look back at the rows of archer he shouted, "You have done well my archers, now please don't slack as we engage, we are counting on you!"

Then with a wave, he galloped to the head of his army. Dismounting he was soon met by some men to help him into a breast plate, helmet and a shield, he then drew his sword. Before he had moved much further he heard a horse approach at speed, looking up he saw Prince Sebastian.

"I wish you would reconsider Tagan, you are a cavalry man," Sebastian said.

Tagan looked at him without expression. He knew this conversation was going to happen since he told Sebastian his plan the evening before.

"I am a soldier first and the leader of this army so I will lead my men from the front so they can see me and if that means joining the infantry I will be an infantryman."

"But you are more use to your army commanding it from behind," Sebastian replied weakly.

"If the Champion Lord can lead his army from the front rank, I think I can do likewise close to the front with my infantry, now please return to your position before you are taken with us." Tagan did not look back as he walked through the ranks of infantry to his position just behind the standard in the fourth row. He gave a reassuring smile and wards of encouragement to all those surrounding him, but in his stomach, he could have been sick.

*****

Peering over the top of his square shield, Tim could see the chaos within the creature's ranks, and he felt sick to his stomach. Tim then heard the words, "Ready to advance." They sounded calm and deliberate as if coming from another world, but as the surrounding Wildbloods tensed their posture, he realised they were his words. How could he sound so calm when he felt so terrified?

"ARMY ADVANCE!" Together they moved forward, one step at a time. It seemed too slow but soon the first line of creatures filled his limited view. The avalanche of arrows did not let up for a moment, just slightly moved ahead of them.

Suddenly, the creatures jumped to face them, as if caught by surprise by their slow movement, and then it began. Tim pushed forward - his interlocked shield in his left hand and his small sword in his right hand. He jabbed with his sword, sometimes feeling nothing but more frequently feeling resistance, before quickly withdrawing his sword. Soon even the handle was sticky with thick warm blood. The ground became uneven as the advance continued, trampling the fallen enemy beneath them.

It was dark, hot and stinking work, and not totally one sided as he noticed the odd hole suddenly appear in their ranks, just as quickly filled by another Guardian, but all the time the slow advance continued, deeper and deeper into the heart of the army of creatures.

*****

Tagan felt butterflies in his stomach as he stood waiting for the order to move, he was not an infantry officer so was leaving the command to someone more experienced in that field, but he hoped his presence would encourage all around.

"Advance, walk forward." Tagan heard the order from somewhere ahead, then together, everyone began to walk forward, not slowly but as a good steady pace together, keeping their ranks and spacing. The mood seemed buoyant as they walked in the morning sunlight. Tagan watched the ranks of creatures grow larger and larger as the distance between them diminished.

"CHARGE!"

"AAAGH!" A great row went up from all around him, Tagan like everyone ran forward, screaming at the top of his voice. Very soon Tagan could hear screams of a different sort, sharper more desperate screams, the fighting had begun!

Smashing his shield forward, he collided with the first creature, bringing his sword down with all his strength he cut into its scally skin. The creature went down and Tagan raised his sword for the next encounter not looking back at his first victim. Clash after clash but Tagan kept driving on, around him both soldiers and creatures fell, victims to their own personal battle.

Tagan soon began to feel exhausted with the weight of swinging both his shield and sword, sweat dripped down his face, occasionally blocking his eyes, yet he could not take a break as that was the very time you were most vulnerable! Casting aside his shield he swung his heavy sword using both hands. He did not let anything come within striking distance. He knew this was working from the screaming in his ears from the creatures he encountered and the ever increasing splattering of blood on his clothing mixed with sweat.

Tagan heard far off to his side a sound he could only describe as rustling, followed immediately by the screams of agony from the creatures, again and again this happened, then suddenly the creatures fell back. Tagan like every soldier around him took only a second to react. They charged forward to join the fighting with the creatures, the sun was now high in the sky.

*****

BANG, BANG, BANG. The heavy knocking on the outer chamber door immediately woke Faith from her slumber with a shock, glancing towards a window she could hardly make out any light, it must still be night, or at the very least, early morning.

The knocking was repeated four more time before she felt dressed and prepared to face whatever crisis had been bought to her door. Opening it, she was slightly surprised to find Berberdoff standing in the corridor alone. She never had him down as a man to make such a display.

"Good morning, Berberdoff," she said sweetly, "and what is so important to wake me in such an abrupt fashion and at such an hour?"

"I'm sorry, Royal Princess, but I thought I should warn you that the battle has begun." He replied breathlessly indicating that he was concerned that the information was important. It took Faith back a little, she knew it was coming but the thought of it was still shocking.

"No, you#re quite right - it is important and yes, I do need to know. Has our Army been put on alert?" he asked.

"Yes, as soon as we heard," he replied.

"Good, I'm going to the viewing platform, would you care to accompany me?"

"Yes, Royal Princess I would be honoured to accompany you." Without another word the pair of them quickly, but not rushing walked to the viewing platform.

The cold morning chill took Faith's breath as soon as she walked out onto the platform. The sun was rising from behind her casting shadows over the view below them. The light was sufficient for them to see the full panorama of the battle laid out in front of them. She watched as the Allied Armies moved toward the swarm of creatures from several different directions. Although it was hard to make out close details from the distance of the viewing platform, it came as an unpleasant shock when the armies collided, then she could hear the screams of the wounded and dying. She felt a little sick at the sound.

But to her surprise she was also fascinated by the horror unfolding in front of her - the spectacle of the fight of life and death, then she felt disgusted with her eagerness to watch the display as the sun rose and the battle unfolded.

"Majesty," Berberdoff's voice broke through her thoughts, "I think it would be an idea for me to find those tunnels about which Chancellor Becket spoke. If that battle goes wrong or if it moves into the Dark Forest, we may need them."

Faith immediately spun around to face him, forcing herself from the sceptical before her. "Good idea, I will accompany you." Without waiting, she walked quickly from the platform with Berberdoff hurriedly following her.

She hardly noticed the almost deserted corridors as she deliberately walked towards where Becket had said the entrance was and she also did not notice the small guard that joined them. The door which hid the tunnels was very non-descript, she had walked passed it thousands of time without noticing it. It opened with ease which made Berberdoff comment that it must be in regular use. Two soldiers of the guard went first, and then Faith and Berberdoff followed with the other two soldiers following up the rear. The tunnels were wide and the ceiling quite high, the floor was stone with wooden panelling on the walls and ceiling, lanterns at regular intervals made it light and airy.

As they walked steadily along, Faith was struck by how quiet it was, their footfall did not even echo. As they moved deeper into the tunnels, Faith felt more and more nervous. Looking at Berberdoff's face, she could see he was feeling the same, but their guard seemed confident which reassured Faith, her army had come a long way in such a short time.

Soon dark corridors began to appear that ran off the main tunnel. Then she noticed large solid doors to each side, most were closed. If this was a place to keep people there looked very little way of escape. Some doors were open, revealing large dark rooms. Faith tried to peer into one of them as they walked slowly passed. Not stopping or going too close she could see something on the far wall which could have been a simple bed and a few objects which she could not make out hanging from the ceiling.

"This looks like a place to keep prisoners, and even torture them!" Berberdoff whispered from just beside her. Faith nodded in reply. Then they came across a join in the tunnel, the one they were walking along and two other tunnels went off in opposite directions, the small party stopped and looked both ways. Both tunnels were lit and appeared identical in every way, some corridors running off them, doors to each side some open some not.

"Which way now?" Berberdoff asked. "Would you like to take two of the guards and search one way and I'll take the other two and go the other? That way we can finish this in half the time."

"No," Faith said quickly. "I would prefer us all to stay together. I am beginning to feel a little apprehensive at what we may discover. This place does not feel right."

"Alright," Berberdoff replied, "then it does not matter which way we take, we will have to come back to check out the other unless of course it takes us around in a circle, and yes I know what you mean, it is making me feel uneasy."

Faith nodded to the right tunnel, and the small party slowly set off again, but Faith did notice her soldier guards, although alert and ready did seem a little more on edge as if they were ready to fight some unknown enemy at any time.

They continued along, not seeing or hearing anyone. Each time they came across a junction they took the right turn, Berberdoff said it would be simpler to navigate back if they always went the same way, as there were no differences in the tunnels to mark them apart.

Faith was beginning to regret her decision to accompany Berberdoff on this quest to discover the tunnels, which she immediately retreated, this needed to be searched and of everyone in the Dark Forest she had the least to do now the battle had begun, and if the worst happened she would have to hide her people somewhere.

"Did you hear that?" Berberdoff suddenly said grabbing her left arm at the same time. The guards had certainty heard something as they tensed up weapon out scanning the surrounding corridor. "I'm certain I heard a very faint voice."

"I heard it too, Sir. I think it came from further up that way," the guard who had been at the front said pointing down the corridor said. Together, without a word, the small party edged its way further along the long tunnel, then on the left they saw a slightly open door with just a glow of light coming from the crack in the ajar door. The soldiers moved silently but quickly to the left side of the tunnel with their backs against the wall, Faith and Berberdoff joined them. Then without a word but just hand signals among the guard a plan was set up, two guards would carefully and silently move along the wall to look into the room, if it was safe they would indicate for the others to join them.

Faith could feel her heart pounding as she watched the two soldiers edge forward, she was amazed no one could hear it, it felt so load and hard. As the two soldiers neared the slightly open door hand signals were exchanged between them. Then one slightly moved out from the wall. He must have been looking to see if he could make out the contents of the room without disturbing the door. A shake of his head indicated to the other one he could not, so this soldier then edged closer to the door and with an out stretched arm used the back of his hand so slowly push the door open further. The other soldier craned his neck to see around the slowly opening door, then with the slightest nod of his head both soldiers quickly disappeared into the room.

Faith gasped an involuntary breath and held it for what seemed forever. There was silence from the room into which the two soldiers has burst, giving no indication as to what they had found. Then one of the soldiers appeared with a worried look on his face and silently beckoned them forward. Faith released her breath.

Inside the room, Faith first saw an old crumpled rag on the floor, a sturdy rough wooden bed without any form of mattress, just wooden slats. Then with a sudden gasp she her eyes fell on a skeleton, hanging by its arms from two chains fastened to the ceiling. How it stayed together Faith could not understand as there seemed to be no skin or muscle to hold the bones in place. It was Berberdoff who acted first.

"Quick," he said to the guards, "help me get him down." With slight hesitation,the guards assisted Berberdoff in unshackling the skeleton and laying it on the ground, the other two soldiers remained at the door alert and on-guard.

Faith looked in amazement at the skeleton. Once it was on the ground, the skeleton began to crawl slowly, using its fingers against the harsh stone floor, towards the bundle of black rags beside the bed, then Faith heard herself say, "Death!" The skeleton stopped from its movement only for the slightest moment as she spoke, but then continued towards its goal. As it got to the bundle it did not stand but continued to crawl inside it, soon the entire bundle was moving as if infested by a hoard of mice. The room was silent, everyone transfixed on the spectacle, even the two guards at the door. Soon, the bundle of rags stopped wriggling and began to rise. Death stood in front of them in the centre of the room and everyone, apart from Faith, unknowingly took a step back.

"Death, how long have you been here?" Faith said, and regretted it as soon as she spoke. Death looked at her with his vacant eyes, and then took two long steps behind her. She spun round to see him pick up his scythe which was leaning against the wooden wall.

"You must leave immediately, there is grave danger here," he said before disappearing into thin air!

"I think that would be a very good idea," she heard Berberdoff say.

Nodding in agreement, she turned to say to him, "YOU, HOW COULD YOU!" Shock and surprise covered Berberdoff's face, Faith spun.

Chapter 22

Mortimer wiped the sweat from his forehead using a dirty blood socked cloth and then his hands, drying them for the next patient as they took away his last silent patient. He had a great deal of hope his last would survive his leg amputation, but the next few days would tell with the heat and lack of water. Infection would quickly spread throughout the field hospital if the dozen or so tents could be called a hospital.

Walking outside to clear his head and breathe some fresh air, Mortimer looked towards the battle being played out to his left. The hospital was quite some distance from the battle so he could not see what was happening, not as he wanted to, it was enough that some of the screams of agony could be heard occasionally and a dust cloud hung over the battle giving away its location. He wished it could be over.

Another stretcher with his next poor soul was bought into the tent and laid on the blood-stained table before him. The table had been scrubbed as clean as possible with fine sand which was what Mortimer now used to clean his hands for the next operation. This poor soul had several abdominal wounds. Mortimer wondered if the man would survive the operation, but he did not decide who lived or died, he just helped as much as he could everyone who was bought before him.

"The creatures have broken through and are heading in this direction, you must evacuate immediately." Mortimer heard a voice say from just outside the open flap of the tent, and then one of the female scout officers stepped inside the tent, beside her was a Trog officer who, from his hot and dusty appearance, looked as if he had come straight from the battle, both looked expectantly at Mortimer.

"I'm a little busy at the moment as you can see," he replied as if the news was as normal as could be, "how far away are they?"

"About two miles at the moment my Lord," the Trog replied.

"Two miles you say. That gives you plenty of time to stop them, or to persuade them to go in another direction," Mortimer said not looking up from his patient. "I have full confidence in your military abilities, but as you can see we are not in a position to evacuate anywhere."

Mortimer did not see the two officers leave. His focus was on the poor man lying on the table in front of him.

"I think he's gone, my Lord," a nurse who stood beside Mortimore said in a quiet voice.

"Yes, I think you're right," Mortimer said as he looked at the lifeless figure before him, "please sew him up and make him ready for burial."

Stepping out of the tent again, Mortimer could hear the fighting was closer, however he was not unduly concerned, in any case with the entire sick and wounded where could they move to? No they would stay here and he would stay with them, but he did start to think of the walking wounded and the medical orderlies and nurses, may be some of them could be moved?

As he stepped back into the hot and humid tent, he saw one of the senior medical orderlies, beckoning her over to him he quickly outlined he's orders for the evacuation, nodding vigorously in understanding and enthusiasm she quickly hurried out of the tent to organise it. Feeling better, Mortimer looked across to the table for his next patient, this young man was a Trog who smiled hopefully up at Mortimer, but his eyes disclosed his pain.

Mortimer worked quickly on his patient, but with care, it was not his intention to make the cure worse than the initial wound, or more painful, but unfortunately that often was the case. He blamed himself for every one of his patients who did not survive the brutality of the operations, but did not gloat in his successes. Every single person who came across his operating table had given enough so far, without making them feel even more indebted to him.

As he finished stitching up his last patient, he felt quite confident he would survive, Mortimer then became aware of a lot of noise outside the tent. Looking up, he saw a lot of worried faces looking back at him.

"What's happening?" he asked.

"I think the creatures have broken through and are in the hospital!" the alarmed reply came back.

Concern and anger were Mortimer's feelings as he brushed the restraining hand off his left arm and stepped out into the dazzling sunlight outside the tent again, what he saw enraged him. Creatures were running amok, chasing down and killing any of the soldiers, nurses or orderlies who were putting up some type of fight. Chronically sick patients who were lying on their stretchers, awaiting their turn for surgery were being slaughtered where they lay. Mortimer felt sick at the sight. Just as he was about to turn away, he heard and then saw a…..

*****

Sylvester studied the large map laid out on the table before him. The hundreds of coloured markers represented all the different parts of his army and that of the enemy. This battle was not just being fought on the ground but in the air above by Titus the fairy, Griffins and Megan with her flying Guardian. This meant Sylvester was supplied with a constant stream of up-to-date reports in real time.

This all came at a cost, of course, as the battle being fought against the flying creatures was as vicus and as bloody as the one on the ground. But it meant Sylvester could oversee the battle like a chess set, better than any of the commanders involved directly in the fighting, and now he was concerned at what he could see developing!

"I want the Guardian cavalry to move into this area and engage the enemy," Sylvester said indicating on the map with a pointing stick. The orders were quickly written down by an officer with responsibility for that area then handed to an orderly behind them. This note was then rushed by the running orderly to the table of the signalling sailors who sent the message by flag or flashing light to the appropriate signalling sailor at the command post for which it was intended, this way orders were given out and responded to almost immediately.

But even with this quick communication, Sylvester was not happy. He could see that after the first initial success the creatures seemed to be gaining the upper hand. Their greater numbers were of course an advantage, but he had hoped to make a greater difference in the early stages of the battle, before the creatures became organised.

A signaller quickly handed an officer who was standing beside Sylvester. Sylvester noticed but took no heed. It was probably another report which would cause the officer to move a piece to a correct place. But no this time the officer suddenly had a sick look on his face.

"Field Marshal, this report states that a large group have broken free and are heading directly to the hospital," he said between his teeth in a low voice. Sylvester looked at him then quickly at the table. The only group who could move quickly to block their path was the Guardian cavalry, but he had just sent them in the opposite direction!

With both hands on the table, he studied the situation, he had to act quickly. "Tell the Mercian lancers to about face and attack the group from the side," he said indicating on the table which direction he wanted them to move, "then the 4th light Trog cavalry can attack from this side." Again, he indicated what he meant on the table, then looking up said "that hopefully will head them off, but just to make sure everyone who has a weapon, grab it and follow me. Captain Summerbee, you are in charge until I return." The little man drew his sword and without waiting for anyone else, ran at an astonishing speed towards the hospital.

Very soon, he could hear the pounding of boots behind him as others caught him up, but he took little notice. His eyes were glued on the horrific view in front of him as the creatures rampaged through the hospital, slashing out and killing helpless patient's lying on stretchers and medical staff, bravely trying to fight back without weapons.

"AAAGH!" Sylvester screamed as he slashed his sword across the back of a very large creature's leg causing it to buckle then he thrust his blood-stained sword into its neck. Not waiting to see the result he searched for his next victim, his blood was up and his anger flared.

Before Sylvester knew it, the fighting was over. He looked around at the dead creatures, daring any of them to move. Then he saw the lancers and Trog cavalry dismounting to help the wounded and check the dead. Looking for his command staff, he was relieved to find none had been killed. Just one signaller had a slight leg wound. Gaining control again, he ordered most of his command staff, the lancers and some of the Trog cavalry back to their original duties. He stayed to see what the butcher's price would be.

As he wondered among the survivors, giving wards of reassurance and comfort where he could, he came across a group of very badly wounded, who all seemed to b transfixed by something they were staring at. "What's wrong?" he asked standing in front of them. "You look like you've seen a ghost?" Without speaking, one of the men just gestured with his hand. Sylvester looked behind and there, not too far away, standing over the crumpled body of some unfortunate person, stood Death.

"Don't worry," Sylvester said to the small crowd, "I think he will have more than enough to worry about without thinking about you."

Walking deliberately across to Death, Sylvester said when he was in earshot, "I suppose you have come to gloat, why you have picked on that particular corpse?"

Death looked up, Sylvester felt a shiver down his spine as Death's eyeless face focused on him.

"I find no satisfaction in futile deaths," he replied from a mouthless skull, "and this body is that of Mortimer."

Sylvester stopped suddenly, he may not have always seen eye to eye with Mortimer, he was a very difficult man to like, but he had saved so many lives with his hospital.

"You are losing the battle!" Death said in a very flat voice. Sylvester was shocked at the words, which in his heart knew were true, but to say it out load and in such a matter-of-fact way!

"So help us," he snapped back, "you're Death, kill some of our enemies!"

"I can't do that, or not in the way you envisage," Death replied, "tell the Champion Lord and Prince Tagan to join me here."

"You say we are losing, and then you want me to call away two of my best commanders in the middle of a battle. I don't care who you are. I am not stupid!" Sylvester screamed at Death.

Death did not react, Sylvester did not think he would, but he felt better for his outburst. But slowly, Death looked back up at him. "I will do what I can to help you win this battle, but I need those two if you want me to help you win the war."

Sylvester looked long and hard at Death. He could not reason if he was speaking the truth or not, he had never understood the trust both Tan and Tim had in Death, but there again, he had never wanted to spend time around him. "Send word to Prince Tagan and the Champion Lord that I need them here as a matter of urgency," he said. To his relief, a voice behind him replied, "Yes sir," before he heard a few horses galloping off. Out of curiosity, he looked behind and saw two of his staff officers and a few signallers.

Turning back to Death, he said, "It will take some time for them to respond."

"I, unlike you," Death said, "have all the time in the world."

As they waited, Sylvester looked all around. The hospital was devastated with nearly every tent pulled down and the few which remained had their canvasses shredded from where the creatures had cut their way in. There was nowhere left to shelter the badly wounded survivors from the burning sun.

Where Mortimer lay showed the carnage of the attack, tables and chairs turned over, all the medical staff had been killed and all the medical equipment scattered everywhere. Now the wounded would suffer even more as there was nowhere for them to get help.

The sound of galloping horses bought his thoughts back to the present. Tagan was riding with an escort of a few Life Guards, away some distance and to his left he could see Tim mounted on a horse with an escort of Guardian, who he assumed would be Wildbloods.

Tagan leapt off his horse without stopping and ran to where Mortimer lay, picking up his head and shoulders he sat down beside Mortimer's body.

"How could this have happened?!" he shouted. But before an answer came, Tim arrived, dismounted slower and without a word walked over and stood looking at Tagan and the body of Mortimer in his arms.

"Give the Champion Lord your sword, Prince Tagan," Death said in a matter-of-fact way.

"Why, how is that going to help?" Tagan asked.

"It is a magic sword Tagan, you must remember that, I hope it may do some magic." Death said softly.

"Do you mean this sword will bring Mortimer back to life?" Tagan said looking up in surprise. "If I stab him with it, the sword will bring him back to life?"

"No," Death said bluntly.

"Then for what reason would I want to give Tim my sword, after all Mortimer gave it to me and that must have been for a reason!"

"Quite so but I do not think in the way you imagine," Death said, "it is a magic sword but you have no magic so cannot use it in that way."

"But I have no magic," Tim said speaking for the first time since his arrival.

"In that I hope you are wrong," Death said.

Gently laying Mortimer's body down, Tagan stood up, he drew his sword, which looked even longer than Sylvester had remembered the blade looking and handed it to Tim.

"I take it you want Tim to do the same thing that Mortimer did to Aaron to turn him into a Golden Griffin," Tagan said, "but you said Aaron was the last Golden Griffin?"

"Indeed, I did," said Death, "but I hope I was wrong, you see I could never understand how Mortimer did that, I'm now hoping I do and this may work." Sylvester had never heard doubt in Death's voice before, and by the look on Tagan's and Tim's faces, neither had they.

Turning to Tim, Death said, "Please, Lord Champion, take the sword and push it into his chest and pierce the heart."

"What will that do?" Tm asked.

"I do not kknow," Death said, "but at worst it will mean Mortimer's body will have another stab wound. At best?"

Tim took a firm grip of the sword handle and carefully placed the sharp tip on Mortimer's chest in the gap between two ribs and adjacent to the heart. Sylvester found himself stepping backwards to give them some room, and then noticed everyone else, except Death was doing the same until there was quite a wide circle surrounding them.

Sylvester saw Tim plunge the sword into Mortimer's chest.

BANG! A clap of thunder and a bolt of lightning studded and blinded Sylvester for a moment. As he began to gain his sight he was astonished to see two arrows of golden fire streaking down from a cloudless sky and strike the ground just beside Tim and Death. Between them stood a Griffin, tall and supreme. The feathers on its wings reflecting the golden in the sunlight as it gently flapped them, its thick fur doing likewise. When it spoke its beak looked bright and golden.

"Death, it's been a long time," the Griffin said. "I thought you had forgotten."

"Zambeese, I was not sure," Death replied, "but I am relieved to see you again."

"Mortimer?" Tim gasped, and the Griffin looked at him.

*****

She felt coldness all over her body, and pain from her arms and wrists. Something was wrong but her head still felt dazed. Trying to open her eyes she could only see very watery blurred figures, but quite a lot of them.

"Help me," she tried to say but no words came out, and then darkness again.

"I'd say you got a very good end of the deal, with a body like that she will keep you warm at night, I'm quite jealous." An unknown voice said from quite close to her, but when she opened her eyes again she could not see who was speaking. What she did see shocked her. Berberdoff was hanging by his wrists which were tied up from the roof, but more than that he was stripped naked, angry red marks showed on his old body and blood was pouring from his mouth and nose.

She realised she was also naked, her hands tied up with rope from the roof, her toes were only just able to touch the floor causing her arms to feel like they were being pulled out of her armpits.

"Well, Princess, you are awake then," a voice said from behind her, but she knew that voice long before Chancellor Becket came into view, his smirking eyes ogling her body, "nice of you to re-join the land of the living."

"You are dead Becket when the King hears of this," she snapped at him through clenched teeth.

Becket smiled at her, then looked at Berberdoff. Shaking his head slightly, he said to Berberdoff, "To think, you bought all your clan to the Dark Forest and put faith in this girl, still we have found some of the best and most enthusiastic volunteers from your ranks, you must be so disappointed."

"You wait…"

"Oh shut up girl," Beckett cut in, "you will speak only when I give you permission, you have a lot to learn as my wife." Faith could hardly believe her ears, her mouth dropped open in shock, but no words came out, her head was in a spin.

"And yes," she heard Becket say, the King does know, who do you think gave you to me?"

The shock of the words almost made her pass out again. Her head was spinning and thumping. Trying to gather her thoughts and clear her head, she heard Berberdoff say, "How long have you had this evil plan?"

"Evil plan, do be serious," Becket snorted in laughter, "the King is just thinking of the future and what is best for his subjects. It is a dangerous world out there over the desert and if we fairies are to take advantage of it and take our rightful place at the top, we must even certain things up."

"So he has given you the Princess as payment?"

"No, no, what do you think the King is, he would not give his only daughter and heir to his throne away. He has just arranged for her to become my wife, that way the line goes on and the King knows his Kingdom is in my safe hands and not those of a gullible girl."

"I am not your wife and never will be." Faith hissed at him. Becket just smiled back.

"So you have created all those creatures, you have bought chaos into the world," Berberdoff said.

Becket looked at him with hatful eyes. "I cannot take all the credit for myself, but yes - I helped, and soon they will have served their purpose when they have destroyed those armies outside."

Chapter 23

"I hope this will work," Zambeese said to Death after finally deciding on a plan. Sylvester hoped it would as well as he walked behind the unusual couple of the spectre of Death and a Golden Griffin.

His armies drew back and parted as he had ordered them to but he was very concerned as neither Death nor Zambeese seemed to know if their idea would work, and Death seemed very reluctant to kill anything, which seemed rather ironic to Sylvester.

"We will need your army to engage the creatures as we do this," Death said, "we cannot do this all alone. Will that be a problem?"

Sylvester shock his head, he wished now he had not let Tagan and Tim go on another mission, which Death had said would end the war.

Death stood about fifteen yards in front of Zambeese facing the creatures, who had now realised that there was a gap and began to move towards it, but before they could move too far Zambeese engulfed Death in flame, Death did not move or to Sylvester's surprise burn in any way, his black tattered robe seemed as normal as ever. But the fire grew hotter and hotter, the flame changed from orange and red to white hot.

Then Death raised his scythe and a bolt of white fire shot out from it and intently incinerated an advancing creature. The creatures stopped, and then another bolt of white fire shot out with similar results. This caused the creatures to panic and run in all directions, this is when the rest of the army engaged them again, but this time the fighting was even more frantic and bloody, the creatures were fighting for their survival and they knew it!

*****

"Where is this entrance then?" Tim asked again.

Tagan was getting a bit annoyed by the repeated question which he had asked about four times in the last ten minutes. Death had said it was concealed but their search seemed fruitless - nothing seemed to be hiding any doors.

"I think we should split up and spread further afield," Tagan said. The Guardian who had come along with them spread out without a word, they did not speak to Tagan, but they did speak to Tim in a language which Tagan did not understand but Tim seemed to cope with it very well, even answer in it.

A call bought every ones attention and Tagan saw a Guardian escorting a fairy, he was one of the fairies who Tagan thought could not fly, but now apparently could.

Ignoring Tagan, the Guardian took the fairy to Tim. Walking over, Tagan could hear the fairy tell Tim where the entrance was, and what had happened to him as he was escorting Faith and Berberdoff.

As Tagan got close to Tim, Tim said, "It looks like the head of the beast is bigger than we thought, Faith has been captured and is a prisoner of Chancellor Becket, I have met him and he is the head of the government, I never took to him and when Titan came and saw me I got the impression he was not too happy with him."

"So will this fairy show us where the entrance is?" Tagan asked.

"Yes," Tim replied, "I think if you take the Guardian and go and rescue Faith, I'll take the others and go and cut off the head."

Hurrying, they found the concealed entrance at the base of a great tree. Anyone not knowing what they were looking for would have found it. Moving into the wide tunnels, it seemed too light for a tunnel. Together, the group silently moved along.

At a junction the fairy came up behind Tagan. "My lord, if I may, I will take the Champion Lord to where he needs to go. The rooms you are looking for are just around that corner and the third door on the left."

Thanking him, Tagan lead his Guardians down the tunnel, he could see no one, but could hear voices coming from the room that the fairy had indicated.

"AAAUGH!" Suddenly, from two fairy soldiers appeared from a door on the left, and a Guardian leapt forward and despatched the two soldiers quickly, but their presence had been detected.

Rushing into the room as the Guardian fought with fairy soldiers who had suddenly appeared in numbers, Tagan's eyes immediately fell onto the naked body of an old male strung up by ropes. He realised it was the fairy Berberdoff. He then saw Faith also Naked and strung up. Before he could move towards her, he saw an old fairy with a long staff which looked like it was a magic weapon. Without waiting to find out Tagan thrust his sword at the old fairy, who jumped back with amazing speed for a man of his age.

Wielding the staff, a bolt of lightning flew out of the end. Tagan stepped aside and struck out with his sword, this time hitting his mark, causing the old fairy to crumple into a dead heap.

"TAGAN!" Faith screamed, he looked at her quickly and saw her eyes wide open behind him at the door. Turning his head he saw two Guardians come into the room.

"Don't worry, they are Guardian, they are with me," Tagan said as he went over to her, cutting the ropes holding her up as she fell into his arms. She felt good and he wished this moment would last forever, but it would not.

Unclipping his cloak, he wrapped it around her. Looking back, he saw that Berberdoff had also been cut down and dressed after one of the Guardian had stripped the clothes off a dead fairy.

"Which is the best way out of here," Tagan asked. Faith pointed down the tunnel and the group slowly moved along it. Berberdoff was also being held up by a Guardian, but he did not appear to be bothered by it. Several times they were attacked by fairy soldiers, but they were quickly despatched by the Guardian. Tagan was beginning to think they were going to have to fight all the fairies in the Dark Forest!

*****

Tim and his Guardians were also making slow progress, some of the fairy soldiers fought fanatically to the very end, others realising that Tim and the Guardian being shown the way by a fairy seemed to realise they were on the same side.

Around another corner and into yet more tunnels, Tim noticed an open door down the corridor on the opposite side. He sensed a tingling all over his body, for some reason he could not explain he knew this feeling was the result of some very strong magic being performed. It was coming from the room with the open door, in which a very old Fairy had appeared. The Fairy's expression suddenly turned to shock as the Guardians became visible to him.

The next moment it was Tim's turn to be shocked as in the open door, above the old Fairy's head, appeared the head of a creature peering into the corridor.

THUD, THUD! Both heads vanished in an instance as two arrows suddenly impacted onto the open doorway where their heads had been. These had been released by the two Guardians who now had now their bows ready again. Running down the corridor they just reached the open door in time to see the last of the occupants disappearing through a door at the far end of a very large room.

The tingling which Tim could sense was almost overwhelming here. He looked at the contents of the room. It was a workshop for making weapons, but not just normal weapons but arrows - golden arrows! They were stacked in bundles just waiting for collection, hundreds of them, and casts of arrows waiting to receive the molten gold, but there was no heat inside the room. The whole process was done by magic.

"I always knew there had to be more to these arrows than meets the eye and suspected that the Dark Forest had something to do with it," Tim said almost to himself.

"Does that mean we are mistaken and the Fairies are also our enemy and serving the Destroyer?" a Guardian asked. He had been stood next to Tim and obviously heard what he had said.

"No," Tim replied, "or rather not completely. Some Fairies are helping the Destroyer who I think is controlling the creatures. All Fairies are able to do magic but most do not realise it, this is old magic, and very strong, only a few can do this, and those are the Destroyer's lieutenants."

"But the Lady Champion does not do magic, my Lord, surely we would if she did?" Tim was asked.

"Every time she flies she performs magic, she has wings and she is quite light in weight, but without magic they would never be able to carry her body weight in flight. Unconsciously, she is performing magic every time she flies, just like all the other Fairies from the Dark Forest. It comes so naturally to them they do not realise it. But some older Fairies are able to control the magic, and under the Destroyers lead have abused the fact for their own benefit."

Chatago, one of his more senior Wildbloods who had been standing beside Tim and listening to what he was saying, asked, "So who is the Destroyer?"

"The only one who could command the loyalty of the older experienced Fairies - The King of the Fairies, who is, of course, Faith's father and Megan's uncle, and the only way we can finish this is by killing him, which is what I intend to do!" Tim said in a determined voice.

"My Lord," a Guardian shouted from around the corner which lead to yet another corridor, "I think we have located a doorway which we believe leads into the main living apartments of the palace."

Smiling at Chatago, Tim said, "Let's go and find the head of this snake!" Rushing towards where the Guardian had indicated the opening to be, Tim saw a door not much different from the hundreds of other doors within tunnel system, but this was slightly ajar, and through the crack could be seen the elegant walls and ceiling of a luxurious corridor.

When they stumbled out of the tunnel system into the main royal corridors, they met the Royal Guard, these were still fairies, but a lot better trained and much more intent in doing their duty, and giving nothing away to the intruders, irrespective of whose side they may be on.

"Why are you fighting us, are we not on the same side?" Tim said to the squad of Royal Guard in a slight lull that appeared in the vicious fighting as the two sides faced each other.

"We are on no side," a fairy said, who was front and centre of the Royal Guard, "we are here to protect the Royal Family to the very end, with our lives if needed. Your very presence shows me your intent is to do them harm, so we will not ask questions but stop you."

"We have a job to do, which we hope will end this war," Tim said.

"Not at the expense of anyone we are guarding!"

There was nothing for it. Tim had tried to be reasonable, but it now seemed a fight to the death was imminent with the fairy guards. Raising his sword, he bought it down with all the force he could muster, but it was blocked. Jump right. Slash left. The bloody deadly dance went on. PAIN! Tim felt it and looked down, he had a deep cut on his left side, blood gushing from it, looking up in horror he saw the fairies' sword coming towards his head closing his eyes he braced for the impact.

Suddenly, he was toppled to the floor by a great weight. Pain raked through his body from the wound. An agenizing scream filled the air.

Silence. Tim felt the weight holding him down but heard nothing. He opened his eyes and the dead fairy's face was looking right into his. His open dead eyes blankly staring at him. Tim jumped up and saw Chatago, one of his more senior Wildbloods, push the body out of the way.

"My Lord Champion, I hope you are well?" he said but then his eyes fell on Tim's open gushing wound. The oldest and wisest of the Wildbloods was sent for, and quickly arrived. Titamay fulfilled for the Wildbloods and the rest of the Guardian the same healing role that Mortimer had, but

Tatamay's methods were far older and most secrets lost in the midst of time.

As Tim lay there, he found they were just as painful. As Titamay worked on Tim, he could see the other Guardian opening doors and searching rooms, from some came the sound of fighting, but others were left open to show they had been checked but undisturbed.

"My Lord Champion, I believe we have found the source of the evil," Chatago said to Tim as he returned with some Guardian.

"Have you dealt with it?" Tim asked.

"No, my Lord, I thought it would be more appropriate if you attended. I have several Wildbloods guarding it. So after a few more minutes of painful treatment, the bleeding had stopped, it was still very painful but with help he was able to get up and walk.

They went a little further down the corridor and into an open door on the left, this revealed a great room, which looked like a living or reception room, bodies of fairy guards scattered over the floor and furniture showed the verbosity of the fighting which had occurred, but then Chatago lead Tim through another door on the far side of the room, this opened into another large and if anything more grander room, but still the bodies of the fallen scattered on the floor, and then threw another door on the far wall into yet another room, this was a bed room with a large four poster bed dominating the room. This was also very grand and had a few bodies on the floor, but what caught Tim's attention was the very old wrinkly man in the bed, either side stood a very wary looking Wildbloods, weapons ready for instant action.

"Who is this?" Tim asked as the old man cast his old peaceful eyes over him.

"This is the King of the fairies and Faith's father," Chatago replied, "but we would know him as the Destroyer!" Tim was taken aback at how such a harmless vulnerable old man could be the Destroyer, if anything he felt disappointed, even cheated.

"How do you know this man is the Destroyer, what proof do you have?" Tim asked.

Chatago lead Tim out of the bedroom through yet another door and across a corridor into another room, in this room which was dominated by a very large and dark table, surrounded by chairs on which where sat dozens of other old male fairies. But it was the feeling of highly-charged electricity in the air that alarmed Tim.

"Can you feel that, Chatago, it feels like someone is preforming magic?" Tim said.

"No, my Lord," Chatago replied, "I can feel nothing, but I would assume they are all preforming magic."

Chatago went on to explain to Tim that they had found out that this room was a part of a secret society founded by a Chancellor Becket and lead by the King. They did not know where Chancellor Becket was but the King was next door and if they wanted to finish the war, that was who they had to deal with.

"Do you think the King would be willing to make a deal?" Tim asked, expressionless faces looked back at him from around the table, and no one spoke.

"Why would he want to make a deal?" Chatago said. "They are winning. Just because we are standing here does not change the fact that the Destroyer's creatures are winning and they know it," he indicated to the old fairies sitting around the table. "e must do something drastic to break the like between the Destroyer and those creatures."

As Chatago spoke, Tim had been watching the faces of the old fairies, as the explanation went on, concern and in a few even panic seemed to run across their faces. Feeling empowered he suddenly realised what he had to do.

"Help me back into the bed chamber. I need to see the King," Tim said and two Guardians help him with Chatago following close behind. Inside the bed chamber standing unaided he drew his sword, a look of concern shot across the old King's face.

"You are about to abdicate in favour of your daughter Faith," and with that Tim swung his sword and in one swift and silent movement decapitated the old king where he sat. Even the Wildbloods looked shocked but Tim said in way of explanation. "We could not kill all those old fairies in that room, so I just cut off the head of the beast."

*****

Sylvester looked in astonishment as suddenly thousands upon thousands of creatures just collapsed dead. He looked over towards Death, who was now returning to his normal black self, as Zambeese stopped breathing fire at him on seeing the creatures fall.

Turning, Death walked over to where Sylvester and Zambeese stood and in his seemingly effortless way he said, "It's over."

Epilogue

Queen Kathryn lifted the young prince up in her arms for the crowds gathered below on the balcony to get a better look. Beside her stood Prince Sebastian looking every bit the picture of a proud father. The Queen smiled at him and then towards the crowd, it had been his idea to show the people of Mercia their future King on Enlightenment Day, the day when Mercia and for that fact most of the world celebrated the delivery from the darkness of the Destroyers Creatures.

This was the fifth year it had been celebrated as for the first time since the war Queen Kathryn had her new sister-in-law Queen Faith of the Dark Forest and her new husband Prince Tagan. As well as all the good and the great who Mercia owed a great debt to were Field Marshal Roderick Sylvester and other commanders from the Allied army.

Queen Kathryn was a little upset that there was no Guardian there, but the Champion Lord and his Lady wife were there, along with their two children, a boy and twin girls. The Guardian, she had been told by Tim, had returned to the land from which they had originally come from.

Handing the young prince to Prince Sebastian to hold up for all to see, she said, "My people, I give you Prince Aaron, your future King."

About The Author

Paul Davies is dyslexic and suffers from multiple sclerosis. Born in Germany to a forces family, his schooling was very disruptive attending seven schools. He was also found to have been born tounge-tied, which was corrected by an operation at about age seven.

At about the age of twelve, Paul was first taught to read, but he left school at sixteen with no useful qualifications. The same age he joined the Royal Air Force, serving for 23 years in at several different stations in different countries. He also saw active service in Northern Ireland the Gulf war and Bosnia, with both the United Nations and NATO. It was also in the RAF Paul discovered he was dyslexic.

Having completed his RAF service, he joined the Police, which he still serves in, but in a restricted role since his being diagnosed with MS.

Paul lives in Stafford with his wife of over 30 years and his two children.